Nellie Nova

Takes Flight

By: Stephenie Peterson

Illustrations by: Elie Dagher

DEDICATION

For my Grandma Ann, who showed me what it means to be a strong woman.

For Keagan, Eden, and Aviel. May innovation run through your veins, confidence beat in your heart, and may joy envelop your soul.

ACKNOWLEDGMENTS

I couldn't have done this alone. I am unbelievably blessed to have some amazing people in my life.

Elie, you helped me bring Nellie to life. I will never be able to thank you enough for creating the art that completes my story. Thank you.

Liz Byer, thank you for your editing genius. You helped my story shine.

Thank you to all of my beta readers, your input helped more than you know.

Katie, thank you for countless phone calls and brainstorming sessions, for talking me through anxiety attacks when I didn't think I could do it. For just being you. You are such a wonderful friend. I am so glad that we haven't let a little thing like 2,887 miles get in the way of our friendship.

Mom and Dad, for better or for worse, you taught me to believe that I can do anything- even fly off the front porch.

My wonderful husband, Nick- you have supported me from day one. We've been through a lot in ten years. Three states (two of them twice!) many, many homes, late nights, 43,942 doctor's appointments. Joy, pain, tears and laughter. I would not trade it all for anything. I love you forever, even if you stink at Scrabble.

PROLOGUE

Nellie could not believe that all the events of the past few weeks had led to this. She'd been kidnapped! After all her hard work, all her time, dedication, and innovation, there she was, stuffed in the backseat of a car, handcuffed, and gagged.

Fear filled her small frame and a thought crept into her mind.

If she had the chance, somehow, to undo everything she'd done, never to have traveled in time, but to be safe at home without fear of something like this happening again, would she do it?

She looked around, taking it all in—the large, scary men who'd taken her hostage, the feel of the metal handcuffs digging into her wrists. The sense of dread as she wondered how on earth she would ever make it back home. It was the most terrifying experience of her life, and she had no clue how to get out of it.

She took a deep breath, thinking about the spiraling, beautiful maze that is eternity, about the people she'd met and the places she'd seen. She wistfully contemplated all that she could see again if she could just find a safe way to get to her family.

Would she give up all that she'd discovered to avoid this moment?

Not a chance in the world.

CHAPTER ONE

Nellie Nova appeared to be a normal girl. She typically wore blue jeans and T-shirts, most often purple ones because purple was her favorite color. She was thin and a tad bit short for a nine-year-old. Her hair was quite often an unruly sea of tangled blond curls, because she was too busy playing to stop and primp. Freckles scattered across her nose and cheeks as if someone had sprinkled a jar of cinnamon over her face and the bits of spice had made a home upon her skin. She wore plastic, rectangular-framed glasses, which were, of course, purple.

Nellie was extraordinary, and that's why she's the hero of our book. Nellie was absolutely brilliant.

She was a girl who knew she could do anything if she just tried hard enough. Above all else, she was strong. Would you ever imagine that a young girl could have more strength than grown men? I'm not saying she could lift a car over her blond curls. Physically, she wasn't especially impressive. It's her inner strength that will shock you. You see, Nellie Nova was . . . Well, let's not get ahead of ourselves. Why don't I start at the beginning? I've been told that it's a good place to start.

Nellie lived in a smallish old house on a quiet street in a quiet town that wasn't too far from a big city, where her mother, Annie, worked as a botanist in a research lab. (A botanist is a scientist who studies plants.) The house was painted sky blue with bright green trim and a sign that read "Casa Nova" hung crookedly over the front door. (If you didn't know, "casa" means "house" In Spanish.) Bejeweled stepping-stones made a twisted path through the numerous plants in the front yard. Several garden gnomes stood guard in the yard, popping up between ferns and hiding among flower beds. There were so many plants, visitors often got the feeling they were walking through a well-planned jungle. Tendrils crawled in every direction, creating a tangled maze of beauty and wonder. An ivy-covered archway separated the front yard from the back. It was made of recycled machine parts: gears, an old exhaust pipe from a car, bike chains, and a variety of other oddities, welded together. Beyond it, the backyard was every bit as eccentric as the front. The backyard teemed with the vibrant colors of every variety of plant imaginable. A tall oak tree dominated the center of the yard. At the top of the tree sat a tree house painted all the colors of the rainbow. A tangled bed of ferns and tall grasses sat below the tree, showcasing more of Nellie's mother's gardening handiwork.

Inside, the Nova home glowed with joy and life There was not a single white wall in Casa Nova. Each room danced with vibrant hues. Houseplants blossomed from every nook and cranny. But that's not what people usually noticed when they visited. What stood out to most people when they entered

Casa Nova was that it was filled with books. Books about science, nature, art, history, and just about anything else you might ever need to know about. Shelves lined the halls, loaded from top to bottom with books, and each wall in Nellie's parents' bedroom was loaded with more shelves with more books. This wasn't just part of the Nova family's taste in decorating. All the books got a lot of use. Everyone in Nellie's house was basically a genius.

Nellie had a brother, Niles, who was eleven. He was a jokester. He loved to play elaborate pranks on people (usually Nellie). Because Niles was so bright, his pranks tended to be on a much larger scale than typical big-brother mayhem. A budding chemist, Niles once doctored the formula of Nellie's bubble bath, resulting in what Niles called "Operation Bath Bomb." When Nellie squirted some of the liquid from the bottle into her bath, instead of creating a layer of foam on top of the bathwater, the solution caused the tub to quickly overflow with a sea of tiny bubbles. Within seconds, the suds multiplied to the point where the room was encased from the floor to the ceiling. Nellie literally swam in bubbles until she made her way to the door. When she opened it, bubbles spilled into the hallway and flowed all the way to the front of the house. Niles was full of mischief—brilliant, naughty mischief.

But don't let his tricks make you think he wasn't a pretty great kid. He may have played a lot of pranks, but he had a kind heart. He adored his family, and he spent his free time volunteering at his local soup kitchen. Niles was full of surprises.

Yes, all the members of the Nova family were quite smart, none more so than Nellie. She learned to read when she was two years old. She built her first robot at three and a half. She knew her multiplication tables at four and half. She began computer programming at five and three quarters, which she likes to point out is three months earlier than her brother, who started right after his sixth birthday. By nine years old, Nellie was studying quantum physics for fun. She thought calculus was a blast. Sometimes, when she was bored, she'd read some of her father's scientific journals, which she found utterly fascinating.

Nellie and Niles were homeschooled. They spent countless hours reading countless books. Nellie liked to do her schoolwork in their tree house in the backyard. Up there, alone with her books, the birds, and fresh air, she often got lost in her reading. Her parents would frequently have to beg her to come down for dinner. Nellie and Niles also often worked on various science and art projects, and they traveled a lot with their parents. They were always learning.

Nellie's dad, Fox, was a physicist, which means he was a scientist who asked questions about matter and energy, and tried to answer them with really cool experiments. He worked from home for the most part but, three days a week, he taught classes at the local university. Nellie and Niles often went to work with him. They'd sit in on his lectures at the university or hang out in the student union and do schoolwork while they waited for him to finish his classes. Often, they'd attract a decent amount of attention, being so young and hanging out on a college campus. The students would stop to talk to them, and before long, Nellie and Niles would find themselves in a debate about philosophy or quantum physics. The Nova kids loved every minute of it.

Nellie loved to learn. She also loved soccer, dancing (though she was always very nervous when the time came for her recitals), participating in Girl Scouts, and painting. That is what she was doing the day our story starts. It was a sunny Tuesday in September and Nellie was sitting in her room, painting a picture of a beaver with extremely large teeth and purple glasses, when her brother burst into her purple-walled bedroom.

"What are you doing?" he asked with a smirk. Niles had an exceptionally memorable smirk. It was easy to tell when he was up to no good. A combination of joy and mischief spread across his thin lips and his freckled face shone with glee under his fiery-red hair.

Niles, like any respectable big brother, was thoroughly convinced that he ought to tease Nellie as often as possible. Don't get me wrong: He loved his little sister, and woe be it to any child who picked on her at the playground, but at home he liked to try to push her buttons.

"I'm painting. What's it look like?" Nellie said without looking up from her purple art table.

"Oooh, silly wittle girl and her wittle girly painting! Girls are so goofy. It's not like this is important. In fact, I don't think any girl has ever really done anything important!" Now, Niles did not believe anything he was saying, but, as I said, he liked to irritate his sister for sport.

"Niles! Of course they have. Think of Mom. She's a

really successful scientist, and she takes care of us. She's totally important."

"Yeah, Mom's great and all, but did she change the world? Show me one woman who's changed the world. Einstein changed the world. Martin Luther King Junior changed the world. Abraham Lincoln changed the world. All guys, naturally," he said with a wink and left her room before she could point out that history is filled with amazing women.

At that very moment, a spark was set off in Nellie's most exceptional mind. As an actual spark needs fuel to become a fire, so does a spark in one's mind. This spark was fueled by excitement. It was fueled by passion. It was fueled by a love of science and history. The largest bit of fuel came from something within her as old as time itself: sibling rivalry. That spark was set ablaze almost instantaneously and soon the tiny spark of an idea was an unstoppable fire of an idea, and she knew exactly what she was going to do.

Nellie was going to build a time machine.

CHAPTER TWO

It might seem strange to you that Nellie's reaction
to her brother's teasing was to turn around and try
to create a machine that no scientist had ever been
able to build before. I know that's not what I would
have done. But when Niles said women had never
changed the world, Nellie's mind was filled with the
faces of great women who had come before her.
The faces of Mother Teresa, Rosa Parks, Maya
Angelou, Amelia Earhart, Sandra Day O'Connor,
Marie Curie, Jane Goodall, and many more amazing
women swam through her mind like a school of
tuna fish, so numerous that there was no end in
sight. As all these world-changing women flashed
before her eyes, she knew she had to meet them.
She knew with their help she could prove to Niles—
and people everywhere—that girls are strong,

smart, and able to make a mark on this world.

The practical fact of the matter was that many of these wonderful women were, well . . . dead. Since she couldn't simply email them, Nellie decided that she wouldn't let a little thing like time get in her way. She'd recently read a scientific journal her father had left in the kitchen that stated that some scientists had said time travel is not outside the realm of possibility. She hadn't thought much of it at the time, but now, with a sense of determination filling her small frame, it all came back to her with a rush of excitement.

Now, I cannot fully describe the inner workings of Nellie's brain, but I can tell you this: The inside of Nellie's mind was a magnificent place. Mathematical equations swirled around in purple puffy clouds; ideas were spoken audibly in three languages; schematics for inventions seemed to draw themselves in midair with an invisible pencil, which left a trail of shining purple glitter as it moved. Pages of giant books flipped constantly, filling the air with a whooshing sound. A large wall of colorful gears, chains, and other machinery moved melodically to the music of Mozart, which played on in the background all the while. And that's just on a normal day.

The day Nellie got her big idea, her mind was working at one thousand times its normal pace. This would have overwhelmed you or me, but to Nellie it was invigorating. Inside her body, her blood seemed to rush through her veins. Her heart beat ever so slightly quicker than normal. Her skin tingled. She knew that she was onto something bigger, bolder, and more significant than ever before. The idea that there might be complications occurred to her, but she was too excited to be scared.

Nellie locked herself in her room for days, coming out only to eat, drink, use the restroom, and gather supplies. She started with a large refrigerator box she found in the garage, which she promptly painted purple. Then, she raided her father's office for books, articles, and a variety of mechanical pieces she stole from his old projects. She covered her wall from floor to ceiling with blueprints, notes, and articles ripped from scientific journals that she thought might be of use to her. After a few days, she ran out of wall space and started taping notes and schematics over windows and on her furniture. Occasionally, on her infrequent trips out of her room, she'd mumble something about time travel to one of her parents, but she never stopped long enough to truly converse.

One by one, the members of Nellie's family began to worry about her well-being, starting with her mother, naturally, as worrying is what mothers do best. Annie Nova peered into Nellie's room one afternoon when Nellie had not emerged for hours, offering her some kale chips and fresh-squeezed green juice. Annie was a warm, kind person, and that warmth shined through in her appearance. Her honey-blond hair was always glossy and her gray eyes were sweet and inviting. Annie held out the snack to Nellie, who accepted but barely looked up from her sketch. Annie's round eyes filled with concern. She bit her lip and watched as Nellie drew furiously, but she didn't say anything. It wasn't the first time Nellie had lost herself in a project. Annie thought back to the time Nellie had built a model of Victorian London in painstaking detail. Nellie had barely come out of her room for a full week. Or the time she'd decided she wanted to modify their robotic vacuum to also polish the hardwood floors. That was another week gone. Nellie was known for her determination. But Annie couldn't help but think that this time-machine business seemed a bit different. She reluctantly left Nellie to her work.

As soon as the door closed, Nellie pushed aside the glass and plate, freeing up more space for her plans. "I know I'm missing something," she thought. "I bet Niles would have a design drawn out by now." It isn't always easy living in a family full of geniuses. As brilliant as Nellie was, brilliance was expected in the Nova family.

The next person who was struck with a bit of worry was her father, Fox. Now, don't get me wrong, his first reaction as a physicist was sheer pride that his nine-year-old daughter would take on an attempt at time travel with such passion. After five days of Nellie's absence at the dinner table, however, Fox was worried that she'd taken on more than she could handle. As exceptional as she was, she was still a nine-year-old child, and Fox thought that maybe she should go play outside.

"Hey kiddo," he said as he opened the door to her bedroom, his green eyes darting behind his glasses to the walls and windows, which were now completely covered with her plans and inspirational articles. Though he was overwhelmed by Nellie's work, he attempted not to show it. He failed, however, and the look of wonderment on his face made him look almost childlike. He and Niles always looked alike, but in this moment, he looked just like his son. He took a breath and composed himself.

"What do you say we go outside for a bit, kick a soccer ball around, and then head to Fork Chops for a milk shake?"

Nellie didn't look up. She simply murmured, "No, thanks," and went back to tinkering with some fuses.

Fox's shoulders tensed. His forehead wrinkled under his mop of red locks. The hairs on the back of his neck stood up. He couldn't explain why, but he felt a great sense of worry for his little girl.

On day six, Nellie gave her parents a reason to be worried. She was attempting a test run of the time machine. Her plan was simply to go forward in time three minutes. Unfortunately, her machine didn't work. I hate to say it, but the mechanics were not quite in place, and,well . . . it caught on fire. It was a just a little fire but, as fires tend to do, it caused quite a commotion.

Nellie was standing in the time-machine box, hoping to visit the near future, when she smelled smoke. Soon a small poof of smoke shot from the top of the box. When Nellie got out, she saw that it was on fire. As Nellie ran for the fire extinguisher, the smoke alarm went off, and Fox and Annie ran into the room to check on their daughter. They got to the room just in time to see Nellie putting out the flames.

"Sweetheart, I'm not sure this is a good idea," Annie told her.

"Maybe you need a break from all of this, kiddo," Fox suggested.

Nellie was not going to let a small house fire deter her from traveling in time to prove her brother wrong. Oh no. If anything, she was even more determined than ever to get it right. Nellie loved her brother a lot. The Novas had taught their kids the importance of family, and Nellie believed it to her core. This, however, was not the time she was going to let something go. This was the time she was going to prove her brother wrong, fire or no fire.

"Mom, Dad," Nellie began, "I know it seems scary that it caught on fire. But I put it right out. I am being responsible. And I will get it right. I know I can. It's just not ready yet."

Fox and Annie wanted to tell her to stop, but they knew it would be of no use. Once Nellie Nova decided she was going to accomplish a goal, there was no getting in her way. Of course, this is really the only way to get anything done. A person who can fully devote him or herself to their goals is someone who will live their dream. And that's exactly the kind of person Nellie was.

"Promise us that you will be careful, sweetie," Annie said.

"And ask us for help before you try anything too dangerous," Fox insisted.

They sighed and left the room, more worried than ever about their daughter but unsure of what they could do about it. Nellie immediately got back to work. The fire caused damage that she would have to repair.

It took ten days for Niles to start to worry. Niles was not much of a worrier, plus he thought maybe Nellie was avoiding him because of what he'd said, and he figured giving her space was much easier than apologizing. Apologizing is one of those tricky little monsters that is usually totally necessary, but is, more often than not, painful. We humans tend to do all we can to avoid pain, and Niles was no different from the rest of us. He was starting to miss having her around to play with, talk to, and, of course, bicker with.

On day ten, he meekly knocked on her bedroom door. When she didn't answer, he put his ear to the door and listened. The sound of classical music rose to meet his ear. He knew that meant she was thinking, as Nellie always played classical music when she was thinking, but he also knew that he couldn't put off apologizing any longer. He opened the door and gasped.

CHAPTER THREE

Nellie was standing in her purple refrigerator box. Inside the box was a large control panel with numerous knobs, buttons, leavers, and a purple keyboard. A computer monitor was attached to this panel, and different dates and locations flashed quickly on the screen. As impressive as the mechanism was, that's not why Niles gasped. Niles gasped because the box was glowing with a bright green light and spinning rapidly.

"Nellie!" Niles yelled. "What are you doing?!"

Without thinking, Niles jumped into the box. As he did, he bumped a lever. The box began to spin faster and faster. Niles and Nellie cowered in the corner of the box. After they had been spinning for about two minutes, the Nova children's fear floated away and their curiosity overwhelmed them.

Most of us don't understand how time truly works. We're trained to think that it's linear, but it doesn't move in an orderly path, going from one year to the next. In textbooks they make it seem like it is, with all the neat timelines and chronological chapters. It's just not that simple. Time, really, is more like a maze, a never-ending labyrinth, twisting and turning and spiraling upward just when you expect it to drop down. It's a beautiful mess of left and right, up and down, north, south, east,and west and today and yesterday and never all in the same breath.

After spending a few moments waiting in curiosity, Nellie edged toward the opening of the box to peek out. Niles followed. What they saw was truly astounding. Time and space spiraled around them. They saw babies gasp for their first breaths of air. They saw the rings of Saturn. They saw weddings and funerals and war and peace. Beaches and mountains, fire and ice. They watched Neil Armstrong take his first steps on the moon and in the same moment saw dinosaurs walking the earth. All of it was moving so fast they could barely comprehend it, but they dared not look away. Pirate ships sailed past them in a sea of stars. A lion chased a gazelle through a heavenly savanna. Nellie grasped her brother's hand and they looked at each other for a mere second, and both noticed that the other had tears in their eyes. They turned back to the spiraling display to see that the box was quickly descending toward the earth. They moved back into the corner of the box and braced themselves. Nellie and Niles knocked heads as the box slammed into the earth with more force than either child expected.

"What are you doing here?" Nellie asked Niles when they realized they were safe on solid ground.

"What *am* I doing here?" Niles asked Nellie.

"I was going to go meet Amelia Earhart and . . ."

"And what?" asked Niles.

"And prove to you that women can change the world .. ." said Nellie sheepishly.

"You built a time machine to prove me wrong?" Niles asked.

"Well, yes, it's kind of embarrassing." Nellie blushed, making her freckles stand out more than usual.

"And kind of awesome!"Niles said, full of pride for his sister.

Nellie shrugged,and then a shy smile crept onto her face.

"So where are we? Or should I say when?"

Nellie pointed to the screen to indicate and yelped. It read 1892.

"Wait! That's not right. I was supposed to go to 1937."

"Oh no! Would touching this lever disrupt your trip?" said Niles, pointing at the lever he'd bumped when he hastily jumped into the spinning box.

"Yes! Did you touch that? That lever adjusts the date!"

"Not on purpose. But yes."

Nellie sighed a deep sigh.

"Well, there's only one thing left to do," she said after a moment, a smile spreading across her face. "We have to see what's outside!"

CHAPTER FOUR

Hand in hand, they stepped out of the refrigerator box and found that they were in an alley on a cobblestone street. Tall buildings loomed on either side of them, and though it was daytime, a thick smog surrounded them and made it feel a bit dark. Farther down the street, horses pulled carriages full of people dressed in fine clothes. In the distance stood a tall clock tower that seemed familiar to Nellie. "Could it be Big Ben?" she thought to herself. "I think this is London," Nellie said excitedly. Nellie had always been very interested in London, England.

She rushed back to the computer and confirmed

her suspicions. The screen indicated they were in London, in 1892. Nellie squealed with excitement.

"Niles! It's London! In 1892!"

"Wow," he said reverently.

At that moment, the enormity of what they'd done began to sink in. Nellie had successfully built a time machine. They'd traveled over a hundred and twenty years back in and time and thousands of miles through space to this little alleyway in London. They stood and looked down the alley onto the street and admired the hustle and bustle of the city, wondering about the people who went past them, what their lives were like.

"I can't believe we're here," Nellie said.

"Neither can I," Niles agreed.

"Should we go check it out?" he asked Nellie.

"I don't know. I wasn't planning for this," Nellie said. She was torn. She didn't know if they should go out into the street looking as they did. Their clothes didn't fit the time at all.

Just then, two kids dressed in ragged clothes ran through the alley, right past Nellie and Niles, and hid in a doorway. One held his hand up to his lips and said, "Ssshh!"

Nellie and Niles were puzzled, but they quieted down and held still. A moment later some men ran down the main street yelling, "Come back here, you urchins! I know you stole that bread!"

They didn't look down the alley and kept running past. A few moments later, the older child thanked them. He was probably about ten years old. The smaller child looked up at them. She was maybe five or six. She whimpered.

"James, my leg hurts. Take a look at it, will you?" she asked the older boy, who Nellie suspected was her brother, as they both had the same round blue eyes and wild blond curls.

"Let me see then, Ruby." She pulled up her skirt and showed that she had a very bad cut. There was a lot of blood. "Oh this is a spot of bother!" he exclaimed.

"You need a doctor!" exclaimed Niles.

"We can't see a doctor; we have no money," the boy said.

Ruby began to cry.

"Well, it's really bad," said Niles.

James nodded.

"I . . . I can help you," Nellie said and she went back into the time machine. She came out with her first aid kit.

"You brought a first aid kit?" asked Niles.

"I'm a Girl Scout, Niles. Our motto is 'Be Prepared.' I take it seriously," she said with a coy smile.

"Well, I am glad you do," Niles responded.

Nellie went over to Ruby and took out an antiseptic wipe.

"I am going to clean your wound. It will sting, but it's going to help you get better faster."

Ruby nodded. Nellie took the wipe to the cut, which was about three inches long, and wiped away blood and dirt. She needed a second wipe to really get it clean. Poor little Ruby winced the whole time.

Nellie then pulled out some gauze and tape and bandaged the wound. Then she gave the rest of the gauze to James.

"Change it every day until it's better," she told him.

James nodded. "How do you know all of this? And what is all of it?"

Nellie looked at Niles, who shook his head. She knew she should not tell the truth.

"Our father is a doctor," she lied. "We've seen him help many people. That's called gauze and that's medical tape," she told him, pointing to each item. "The gauze will soak up the blood and the tape is sticky on one side so it will keep the gauze in place. The little wet cloth is called an antiseptic wipe. It cleans the wound."

James and Ruby seemed to accept this as true. James helped Ruby to her feet. She seemed much better now that the cut was bandaged and she'd had a moment to breathe and relax.

"Thank you very much," James said to Nellie and Niles.

"Yes, thank you," Ruby added.

"It was my pleasure," Nellie said.

Ruby and James walked away quickly, heading nervously in the opposite direction of the man who'd been chasing them.

"Shall we take a walk?" Niles said in his best British accent, which, to be completely honest, was not a very good impression of any Brit I've ever met.

"We shall," replied Nellie in an equally bad accent. They started down the alley, but Nellie pulled back.

"Niles, we really should not go out there in our clothes. I want to see London so badly, but this is not safe."

Niles nodded and scanned their surroundings. He saw a trash can and started digging through it. He found some torn up jackets and a boy's hat. It wasn't perfect, but they'd blend in a bit better this way. They happily made their way to the street.

They walked through the city and tried not to inter-act with anyone, to be quiet and unobtrusive. The kids loved seeing all the clothes, the horse-drawn carriages, the different people interacting with one another and a world simpler, in many ways, than their own. No one walked down the street listening to music or chattering away on an iPhone. As a result, they seemed to talk to one another a lot more than Nellie noticed on the streets of her own town.

There was so much to take in. Nellie especially loved seeing the clothing the women wore. She found all of their hats to be quite beautiful. Niles thought that the women's bustles on their dresses were very funny. The bustles made the women's behinds appear to be much larger than the rest of their frame. It was all the rage in fashion at the time, but it was unlike anything he'd ever seen. Niles really enjoyed the top hats he saw a few men wearing. He wondered if he would look silly wearing one in his own time.

There was a dark side to all of it, however. There were so many people who seemed to be very poor, much like Ruby and James. London in the 1890s had a huge discrepancy in wealth between the classes, and people seemed to either have a lot or nearly none. It made Nellie sad to think about all those hungry kids.

They headed back to the purple time machine

quietly. When they were almost back, they saw Ruby and James coming around the corner. Ruby waved at them excitedly, and the four children hurried their pace and met up near a butcher's shop.

"'ello again!" said Ruby excitedly.

"Hello. You seem to be doing better," replied Nellie with a smile.

"I am! My knee feels oh so much better now! Plus we nabbed another loaf of bread. We're orphans. I've been so very hungry," Ruby said loudly.

"Ruby! You need to keep quiet about that kind of thing," said James in a loud, scolding whisper. "You don't know who might hear you."

"You're right," a voice said from behind the kids. "You never know who might hear you."

The four children turned slowly and saw the men who'd been chasing Ruby and James before.

"Run!" yelled James.

The kids sprinted down the alley where the time machine sat waiting for Nellie and Niles. Though they had the urge to jump inside, Nellie and Niles

knew it would not be a good idea with so many people watching. The men were close behind them and screaming at the kids for taking the bread. The Novas, it seemed, were guilty by association.

They exited the alley and ran across a street. Ruby ran slower than the other children, because her legs were shorter. The larger of the two men was a fast runner and caught up to her. He grabbed little Ruby and picked her up.

"Oi! I got your sister, urchin!" he yelled.

James stopped dead in his tracks. He paused for a moment, and then ran back to his sister.

Nellie and Niles just kept running. They turned up a street to get away from the men. Nellie ran as quickly as she could, not looking back at her friends. Though she knew Ruby and James were in danger, she was too scared to try to help. If the men caught them too, they might be found out. Nellie knew they could not give away their secret. No one could know that she and Niles were time travelers. After about a minute, they'd made it back to the box in the alley. They heard one of the men yelling at them from the street to come back.

"What should we do?" asked Niles.

"We go. Now. As far as we can from here," Nellie insisted.

"But, Ruby and James . . ."

"We can't, Niles. No one here can know where and when we come from. The more time we spend around people, the stranger we'll seem," Nellie said sadly.

The shouts from the men grew louder.

Nellie's eyes widened; she shouted at her brother. "Get in," she demanded. "Now."

Niles complied, but he gave Nellie an earful as she

frantically moved the levers around and started the machine.

"It's not right, Nellie! What we did—leaving them. It's not okay."

"Shut up, Niles. We did what we had to do!" Nellie snapped at her brother and immediately felt guilty.

She didn't even pay attention to when or where she'd set the machine to travel. All she cared about was that they left quickly.

The machine lit up. It began to spin. They could still hear the men yelling from somewhere on the street as the machine lifted off the ground and spiraled far, far away. Nellie hoped they hadn't seen the time machine as it took flight and then disappeared into time. They watched the labyrinth of time half-heartedly for a few minutes out the open door of the time machine. They observed screeching monkeys climbing through a beautiful rain forest. They saw people building a skyscraper. They watched in horror as a tornado tore through a cornfield and flattened a barn. They saw so many incredible things, but were not filled with as much wonder as one might think. They were filled with a heavy sadness.

That sadness distracted them a bit from their task. Nellie stared blankly at the flashing computer monitor, absentmindedly watching times and locations flash on the screen, wishing that she would have done things differently. Niles sat down and leaned against the side of the box near the opening and sighed. Suddenly, the time machine made a quick movement and the resulting jolt sent both children flying. Nellie flew forward and knocked her head on the console. She saw black for a second. When she opened her eyes, she turned to ask Niles if he was okay.

But Niles was nowhere to be found.

Nellie blinked. "Niles?" she called out meekly.

"Niles? How could you pick a time like now to trick me? Come out!" said Nellie, thinking he must be hiding. But as she looked around the small box, she realized something.

There was nowhere to hide.

Then it hit her. Niles must have been launched from the time machine with the lurch that caused her to bump her head. Niles was lost in all of eternity. As the reality of her situation began to sink in, Nellie knew what she needed to do. She had to find Niles. It didn't matter where he was—nor when. Nellie needed to search all of time and space until she found him.

CHAPTER FIVE

Screaming, Niles spiraled through eternity. Honestly, to say that he screamed is a bit of an understatement. The sound that Niles made was more of a roar, a vocal explosion of sheer terror. His face contorted as his open mouth stretched farther than you might think possible. Tears streaked down his freckled cheeks and flew off his face into the vast endlessness surrounding him. Niles was sure that this was his end, and he would never see his family again. He was just starting to get sentimental thinking of his mother when solid ground appeared beneath him and he realized that he was about to make contact with the earth. Niles had no way to prepare himself for the fall. He tried to curl

up into a ball, but was unable to do so as he spiraled quickly. He crashed into the ground with such force that he was knocked unconscious on impact. His body was sprawled on the ground somewhere, sometime unknown to both himself and Nellie.

Back in the time machine, Nellie was trying not to panic. She knew that she had to find Niles and find him quickly. But where—and when—could he be?

The machine crashed into the ground and Nellie glanced at the screen to see when and where she was. The screen on the wall of the time machine read, "Paris, France, December 18, 1999." She sighed, thinking Niles would have really enjoyed Paris, when her exceptional mind had an exceptional thought. She'd been looking at the screen the whole time, right up until she hit her head. Maybe, just maybe, he'd fallen out into the last location she'd seen. Inside her mind, the moment replayed like a movie. In addition to her many other gifts, Nellie had a photographic memory. The locations scrolled before her. "New York City, New York, USA on December 20, 1852," "Cape Town, South Africa, on March 29, 2009," "Plano, Texas, USA, on July 21, 2012," "Athens, Greece, on August 28, 1683," "Silverdale, Washington, USA, on April

12, 2007," "Tenochtitlan, Mexico, on March 18, 1505," then THUD, she hit her head on the screen. She hoped and prayed that her theory was right. If it was, Niles would be in the ancient Aztec city of Tenochtitlan.

Without so much as a glance toward Paris, Nellie typed the location into the time machine's computer. Off it spun, into time and space, spiraling, twisting, and turning, hopefully toward Niles.

Niles was lying on the ground, curled up in a ball, moaning unconsciously. He was totally unaware of his surroundings, but if he had been in better shape, he would have taken in the beauty of the great ancient city around him. The sun shone brightly upon his battered body, birds sang sweet songs overhead, and a gentle breeze filled the air. Had it not been for the fact that he was badly injured, it would have appeared to be a perfect day.

After several minutes of rolling around on the

ground in pain, he slowly started to become conscious again. He remembered falling, falling so very far. But where had he fallen from? Then he remembered. He had fallen out of Nellie's time machine and he could be anywhere—and any time. How he wished he were at home, safe in his bed.

Slowly, he forced himself to open his eyes and accept reality. The sunlight was a welcome surprise, as was the beautiful setting. He was sitting on the shore of what appeared to be a large lake. Mountains encircled the lake, and it appeared he was on an island. The island contained a large city full of ornate buildings and many people traveling on dirt roadways and on small boats through canals. He sat up, beginning to panic about what he would do next. This city seemed familiar, but not in an "I've been here before" kind of way. It was familiar in an "I read about this in my history book" kind of way. He wasn't going to be able to find his own way home without Nellie and her time machine.

A heaviness filled his chest as he rose to his feet. What on earth was he going to do? Where would he go? He looked around, searching for somewhere to hide, thinking it might be best if he stayed out of sight of the many people bustling about the city.

As he scanned his surroundings, a shadow blocked out the lovely sunlight. Niles looked up and saw something that filled his heart with joy. Above his head was Nellie's time machine, spiraling toward the ground in all its purple glory. It hit the ground about a hundred yards away from where he was standing. He ran for it, but so did a lot of other people. A dozen or so tan-skinned, dark-haired, shirtless men ran toward the time machine, surely wondering what in the world was going on. Niles' heart pumped with fear as he struggled to get to Nellie before them. He pushed through the pain of his injuries and quickened his pace.

Several of the men were shouting in a language he did not understand. But he didn't need a translator to understand that they weren't happy. A terrible sense of dread overtook Niles.

He pushed ahead of the crowd as Nellie poked her head out of the box and called, "Niles? Oh, Niles please be here!" Quickly, she spotted him. They made eye contact briefly. Nellie saw the crowd running toward them and rushed back to the computer, ready to send the machine anywhere but Tenochtitlan as soon as Niles entered the machine. He burst through the door, and Nellie sent the purple box away.

As it lifted off, they rushed to each other and hugged.

"I thought I'd lost you!" she cried.

"I thought I'd never see you or Mom or Dad or anyone ever again! Thank you for coming back for me."

"Of course. I don't know what I'd do without you."

"Well, thanks. But aren't you hurt? What even happened to you in Tenochtitlan?"

"Nothing really. I was unconscious for most of it. Wait, I was in Tenochtitlan? Those people were Aztecs? Aw man, that would have been so cool if I wasn't so scared! I knew that city looked familiar! I am all right, Nellie. I'm sore, but I'll be okay. It's just good to be safe and with you."

As much as the Nova children could argue, bicker, and drive each other crazy, they loved one another fiercely. They were both relieved to know that they were together again.

Their relief was short-lived, however, because Nellie quickly noticed a problem with the time machine.

Gasping, she pointed toward her feet. There was a

hole in the bottom of the refrigerator box.

"Should we go home?" asked Niles.

"I think we're going to have to!" said Nellie sadly.

She pulled a roll of duct tape out of the backpack of supplies she had stocked the machine with and attempted to patch the hole.

"That should hold us for now, but we won't be meeting Amelia Earhart today," Nellie said mournfully.

She turned to the computer and set the date to "2015" and the location to "home."

"You can fix it, Nellie. I'll help. You'll meet Amelia. I'm sure of it," Niles told her.

The machine's engine whirred, and a component Niles could not identify, mounted above the computer monitor, filled the box with a bright green light. The kids shielded their eyes for a moment and then, stepping carefully over the patched hole, made their way to the doorway of the machine to watch what they hoped was not their last trip through time.

Nellie and Niles eagerly watched as time scrolled before their eyes. While the undulating, startling unraveling of time was quite a spectacle, the reaction going on inside Nellie's sparkling gem of a mind was even more interesting. With every new sight, the gears spun faster, the dancers moved more gracefully, and the music became more and more enchanting. It was truly a wonder to be seen, If only one could actually see inside of Nellie's mind.

The refrigerator-box time machine hit the ground with a jolt. Nellie and Niles were knocked off their feet, but neither was hurt. After a moment, Niles stood up and reached out his hand to help Nellie to her feet. Nellie checked the computer screen to confirm they'd landed in their home on the same day they left. They had, and for this, they were thankful.

CHAPTER SIX

Nellie and Niles were barely able to step out of the box before their parents blustered into Nellie's bedroom.

"What on earth is going on in here?" Fox shouted.

"Nellie! Niles! Are you okay?" Annie gasped.

"Daddy," Nellie began, "I did it. My time machine worked."

Fox's eyes grew wide.

"Niles came with me. First we went to London in the 1890s, and helped some street kids. The little girl fell, and I helped her clean out her cut.

But scary men were chasing them and we had to leave them. Then Niles fell out of the time machine . . . but I found him, Daddy, in Tenochtitlan. He's okay. Really."

Niles nodded, trying to reassure his parents. "It was absolutely amazing, Daddy. You wouldn't believe how beautiful time travel really is. Time's not a line. It's more of a maze. A maze of wonder and beauty."

Fox was overcome with emotion. He was immensely proud of his daughter for actually building a time machine. He was also exceptionally angry with his children for leaving not only the house, but the century, without telling him and Annie.

Annie stood silently for a moment, then rushed

over to the kids and threw her arms around them. She was delighted, furious, and relieved. Fox joined them and threw his arms around his family.

"I am so, so, proud of you," Annie told the kids, "but you are so grounded."

"But, Mom!" Nellie and Niles chorused.

"I built a time machine! By myself!" Nellie said.

"And you left the house without asking!" Annie said.

The kids groaned, but they knew she was right. They shouldn't have traveled in time without talking to their parents.

Fox looked at Nellie, his eyes misty with tears of pride. "I cannot say how very impressed I am with you, Nellie. It's nothing short of amazing what you've done. You wanted to do something and you decided that you would not stop until it was done. You accomplished something that no one who tried before you has ever been able to do. And then you handled it all with bravery and quick thinking."

Nellie beamed. It wasn't easy to truly impress Fox Nova, and it made Nellie very happy to know she had.

Fox looked at Niles. "And you, you took care of your sister and acted responsibly. I'm very proud of you too, Son."

"Thanks, Dad."

Fox gaped at Nellie's purple time machine. He inspected the gears and levers, peered at the computer monitor, and admired the engine. After a few minutes, a smile spread across his face. It was a smile that I have to say was quite reminiscent of Niles's smile when he was up to no good. It was a smile full of mischief and wonder.

"When do I get to use it?" he asked.

Nellie sighed. "Not anytime soon," she replied.

"Well, why not?" he asked.

"It's broken. The box is ripping. It needs a whole new frame. I should have known better than to use a cardboard box to travel through time. What was I thinking?!"

Nellie had a tendency to be too hard on herself. It's hard to live in a family full of geniuses. What Nellie didn't understand—what most kids with loving parents don't get—is that her parents did not expect anything out of her other than effort and kindness. Of course they enjoyed her achieve-ments, but they would not have loved her even one percent less if she'd been any less exceptional.

"Well," Fox said, wrapping his arm around his daughter. "I guess we'll have to fix it."

Nellie beamed. A shiver of excitement shot down her spine. Maybe she'd get to meet Amelia Earhart after all.

CHAPTER SEVEN

For a few hours the following day, Nellie locked herself in her room again, trying to fix the time machine by herself. Niles did not leave her in peace for long. He'd been part of her time travel adventure, and he was not going to be left out of the repair and redesign. Together, they drew up a blueprint of the new and improved time machine. It took several attempts and lots of revision, but Nellie and Niles made a good team and, in spite of the mess they made while working, they accomplished a lot.

By lunchtime that day, they'd worked together to

create a solid plan for the new machine. The only problem was they didn't have everything they needed to make it happen. They found, however, that when they asked their father, who was working on some research in his home office, he was more than willing to take them to the hardware store for supplies. In fact, Fox was almost giddy as they picked up lumber.

When they got home from the hardware store, Nellie and Niles realized that their duo had become a trio. From the moment he'd been included, Fox was hooked on the project. They all worked hard to build a new frame for the machine. It would be solid wood with old tires attached to the bottom to act as shocks. Hopefully, this would make future impacts less bumpy.

Nellie busied herself with painting the frame purple while the guys took a snack break. When they got back, Fox and Niles were wearing identical impish grins.

"What's up, guys?" Nellie asked.

"Niles had the most amazing idea."

"What's that?" asked Nellie.

"I think we should build an invisibility shield of

sorts," Niles blurted. "We can attach mirrors to the exterior, paint the backs purple,but when you turn on the shield, they'll flip over, so that the machine blends with its surroundings. Something mirrored is less likely to attract attention while we're out exploring."

"That's brilliant, Niles!" Nellie was truly impressed.

"Thanks, Nellie."

After another run to the store for mirrors and the electronics required to make them flip, Nellie, Fox, and Niles got busy painting them, wiring them, and attaching them to the time machine. When Annie got home from work, she found the three of them in Nellie's room, talking, laughing,and working together.

"Hey," she said, poking her head into the bedroom. "Is there room for one more helper in here?"

"Of course, Mom!" Nellie said.

Within the hour the shield was built.

"So is it ready then?" Fox asked excitedly.

"Well, I'd like to make some changes to the computer programming."

Fox sighed. His desire to try out the time machine was stronger than that of a child eager to open the gifts under the tree on Christmas morning.

"Give me a day or two, Dad." Nellie laughed.

"Okay. But why don't you take a break? Go play outside with your brother."

Nellie sighed, but she agreed. The siblings decided to take a walk through the neighborhood. When they got outside, they noticed three men in suits sitting in a car across the street. Nellie nudged Niles and asked what he thought of them. Before he could answer, the men drove away quickly.

"They were probably just lost,Nellie." Niles said.

But Nellie was not so sure. A sorrowful song played inside her phenomenal mind and one of the giant books slammed shut. Something was not right.

CHAPTER EIGHT

Nellie stayed up late that night, working hard on her new programming. She wanted to surprise her family with her changes. At about 2:00 a.m., she was finished. She was so excited. She would be able to travel in time again. It had only been a little over a day, and she already missed it. She was even more excited because she'd come up with a plan for where to take her parents on their first trip through time.

Even though she'd been up much too late for a nine-year-old, that morning she was up before the rest of the family. She went into the kitchen and made them all breakfast. There's nothing like the smell of bacon, eggs, and coffee to draw people out of bed.

Nellie's plan worked, and soon her family was gathered around the table enjoying the tasty meal she'd made for them. Annie took a sip of coffee and asked Nellie what was up. She knew that her daughter, although sweet, was not usually the kind of person to get up early and make breakfast.

"We're going back in time today." Nellie smiled.

"I thought you needed a few days?" Fox said excitedly.

"I stayed up late and finished it." Nellie told him.

"All right!" said Niles.

"Where are we going?" Fox asked, nearly squeaking with anticipation as he bounced to his feet. He briefly turned back to his plate to snatch up a piece of bacon for the trip.

"Or when?" Annie asked nervously.

"I'm not telling you. It's a surprise. Don't worry though, I guarantee you will like it." Nellie told them.

Fox and Annie exchanged glances the way parents do when they are trying to have a discussion in front of their kids without speaking. Annie nodded, and Fox said, "Okay then, let's go!"

The family made a beeline for Nellie's room. The moment they entered the room, Fox leaped into the time machine, which now had a working door and eye-level windows on three sides. Annie and Niles followed, and Nellie entered last. She was smiling.

"Good morning, Purple Flyer," she called out in a clear, cheerful voice.

"Good morning, Nellie Nova. Where would you like to go today?" a voice answered from the computer terminal.

Annie gasped and then giggled.

"I'd like to go to the First Church of God on Fremont Street in Harborville, Oregon. On September third, 2003."

"Our wedding?" Annie asked with a smile.

"I figured this is better than watching your wedding video." Nellie smiled back.

"I detect voices that are not Nellie Nova's. Would

you like to add new commanders before liftoff?" the computer asked in a choppy, electronic-sounding voice.

"Yes, please, Purple Flyer."

After a few minutes, all the Novas were registered in the computer's system so that they could command it with their voices. One of Nellie's programming changes included this security measure. That way, no one could move her ship without her approving them.

"Are you ready to go?" asked the computer.

"Yes, Purple Flyer," Nellie chirped.

A green light filled the machine. The engine whirred and the time machine began to spin around and around. Fox whooped. Annie giggled. The machine lifted off.

"Now, you watch," Nellie told them. All the Novas fell silent as they watched time unfold before their eyes.

"You were right," Annie told Nellie after a minute or so. "It's not a line. It's a maze. A splendid, confusing, wonderful maze."

As they watched out the window, the ground

became visible underneath them and then Nellie knew they'd soon come to a stop. "Brace yourself," she called out to her family.

The impact, while not smooth, was much less dramatic than before. The Nova family stood up and looked out the window.

"Welcome to Harborville, Oregon, United States of America. The year is 2003. The local language is English. Do you require more information on the area?" asked the computer.

Niles looked at Nellie and gave her a thumbs-up.

"No thank you, Purple Flyer. We've got this! Please enter invisibility mode," Nellie answered.

"That is going to be so useful!" Niles told Nellie.

Panels turned over on all exterior surfaces of the machine, covering even the windows with mirrors. Fox opened the door, ready to see what it looked like from the outside.

"Wait!" Nellie told him.

"You can't go in there looking like that!"

In their excitement, all the Novas, other than Nellie, had climbed into the time machine in their pajamas.

"Oh no," said Annie with a look of panic on her face.

"Don't worry, Mom," Niles said.

"Do you have appropriate clothing for a wedding?" Annie asked him.

"No, but Nellie does."

Annie turned to Nellie, mouth open, ready to ask how they were going to dress for the wedding, when she realized that of course Nellie would have everything they needed. She smiled at her daugher. "Always be prepared."

Nellie went to a bench they'd built in front of the computer. The seat was hinged, and inside there was room for storage. She pulled out suits for Fox and Niles, and a pink floral dress for Annie. They dressed quickly and Fox started out the door again.

"Not yet!" she told them.

She returned to the bench and pulled out a large hat and a dark wig for Annie, a wig for Fox, and glasses for both of them.

"You can't look like you!" she told them. "No one can know that you are watching your own wedding." Everyone nodded in agreement. Fox and Annie added the final pieces.

Fox looked at Nellie pleadingly. "Now?" he asked.

Nellie smiled and nodded. "Now."

The time machine had landed behind the church. There was not much back there, just a thin patch of grass separating the church from an alleyway.

"No one's coming back here," Niles said.

The Novas walked toward the front of the building, looking down and trying to blend in with the guests. They had five minutes before the ceremony would start.

Fox immediately walked in and found the guest book. He turned to the last page and scrawled "One day, you'll know," without a word. He smiled at Annie.

Annie gasped.

The kids looked at each other, confused.

"What?"

"That message has always been in our guest book. We always joked about what it could be that we'd know someday. Today is the day. Today, we know," Annie said in a reverent whisper.

"Wow," said Niles.

"Let's find a seat," Fox said.

The family entered the chapel, which was decorated with thousands of beautiful flowers. The center aisle was completely covered in white rose petals. Floral garlands were woven between all the seatbacks. At the front of the chapel stood a beautiful archway made up of thousands of white and yellow dahlia flowers. The Novas stood in the doorway for a moment, taking in the excitement, beauty, and sweet smell. Quickly, however, they took a seat in the pew closest to the exit. They waited wordlessly for the ceremony to start, trying not to make eye contact with any of the guests. After a few minutes, Fox entered through a doorway near the front of the chapel with a minister—Fox from twelve years before, young and bubbling over with such joy he looked as if he might burst. Soon music filled the room as the band began to play the "Wedding March."

They turned to the entrance to the room to see
Annie, standing with her father, the kids' grandfather, who had passed away in 2012. The kids
smiled, and tears came to everyone's eyes at the
sight of his face. Annie looked so beautiful in her
wedding dress, and her elation was as obvious as
Fox's.

Nellie had to resist the urge to run up and hug her
grandfather. It was wonderful and awful all at once
to see him. So many feelings flooded the Nova
family: Happiness brought on by memories of good
times with Grandpa. Heartache from the memory
of his passing. Amazement at being able to see him
again. Finally, there was an aching feeling, knowing
that they would not see him again and could not
talk to him. Annie and Grandpa from 2003 walked

down the aisle, and he lifted her veil, gave her a kiss on the cheek, and the ceremony began.

Annie and Fox both had tears in their eyes the whole time. Nellie and Niles loved watching their parents—in both past and present forms—look at each other. The love was obvious in any time period.

Nellie and Niles thought it was fantastic to see their parents so young. They enjoyed looking around the room and seeing all their relatives react to the ceremony. Being able to share this moment with their parents in this way was powerful.

All too quickly, the ceremony came to an end and they watched as Fox and Annie had their first kiss as a married couple. The guests dispersed and made their way to the reception. The Novas held back until the chapel was empty. Annie wiped a tear from her eye and stood up. Her family followed suit.

"I guess we should probably head out," Fox said with a sigh. "I'd love to stay for the reception, but it's not a great idea. Someone may recognize us."

They made their way to the exit quietly. Fox and Annie tried to make a point of keeping their heads down, hoping no one would get a good look at them. They'd just about made it out the door when a voice called from behind them.

"Little girl?! Little girl, you dropped your hair bow!"

Nellie turned around to see her grandfather holding her purple bow. Panic rushed through her for a moment. Then she realized he could not recognize her because she had not been born yet. She walked toward him to get it.

"Thank you, sir," she said, looking deep into her grandfather's eyes.

"You're welcome. What a polite, pretty young lady you are!" he told her.

"Thank you," she said. Then it happened. She hugged him. In spite of everything she'd told herself about not interacting with their family in the past, she just couldn't help it.

"Oh, and affectionate!" He laughed. His eyes twinkled. They always had.

"Sorry," Nellie muttered quickly.

"It's okay. It was nice to meet you."

"You too. Thanks again," she said, her voice a bit

wobbly, and ran back to her family, her heart happy knowing that she got one last hug from Grandpa.

CHAPTER NINE

The Novas returned home just a few minutes after they'd left. Annie headed to work, Fox went to his home office, and the kids went out to the tree house for some reading. Everyone needed time to process everything they'd just seen, despite how wonderful it had been.

Nellie was distracted, however, and was not getting anywhere with her reading. She stared out the window, thinking of her grandpa. Suddenly, she snapped back into reality when she saw them again — the men in suits. This time they'd parked down the street and were standing outside their black town car, pointing at Casa Nova.

"Niles," she whispered.

"Huh?"

"Look," she said, barely audible. "Those men are back."

Niles looked up to see that the men were, in fact, standing down the street from Casa Nova.

"Hmm, that's weird," he said, not sounding concerned. He looked back down at his book.

Nellie, however, kept watching. She could not explain it, but these men sent shivers down her spine. They got back in the car, but didn't leave. They kept watching Casa Nova, and Nellie kept watching them. This went on for about an hour as Nellie watched them point to the house, pass an

IPad back and forth, and talk to one another, eyes always on the house. Nellie couldn't stop watching the men watch her home. Niles just kept reading.

Nellie was starting to lose interest in spying on the spies when one of the men got out of the car again. He walked right up to her front yard.

"Niles!" Nellie said in a voice somewhere between a whisper and a hiss.

Niles looked at her and she nodded her head toward the tree house window. He turned just in time to see the man crouch down in a garden bed and peek inside their living room window. Niles's jaw dropped.

"What is that man doing?" he whispered as quietly as possible.

"I don't know," said Nellie, "but I don't like it."

 They watched as he walked around to the side of the house and trampled over some plants to peek in another window. Then he walked through the archway into the backyard.

Nellie and Niles got down on the floor of the tree house, praying they wouldn't be seen. They could see a bit of the yard through the opening of the floor where the ladder went into the tree house. They watched as the man peeked in a few more windows, stepped on several more plants, and then made his way back to the black town car, which sped away, tires squealing as they turned off of Nellie's street.

"Woah," whispered Niles.

"That was absolutely, positively insane! What was he doing? Did you see the way he just stomped all over mom's plants? And why is he looking in our house? What do they want? I don't like it, Niles."

"I don't know, Nellie. We've gotta tell Mom and Dad."

Nellie agreed. They climbed down the ladder of the tree house and headed inside to tell Fox what they'd seen. When they got there, however, their father started talking excitedly before they could even get a word in.

"Nellie, Niles. Sit down. I've got great news!"

The kids complied.

"I just got off the phone with your mother. We've decided to let you two go ahead and use the Purple Flyer on your own to go meet Amelia Earhart. Nellie, you made that machine specifically so you could do that and we think you should!"

"Really?!" Nellie squealed.

"All right!" said Niles. "When do we get to go?"

"Right now if you want," said Fox, his entire face smiling.

The kids ran excitedly toward Nellie's room.

"Thanks, Dad! See you later!" called Nellie.

"Bye!" said Niles.

Fox sat down at his desk, happily thinking about the adventures that lay before his children.

Neither Nellie nor Niles remembered the men in suits.

CHAPTER TEN

The Purple Flyer whirled through eternity. Nellie was anxious and excited all at once. She'd been an Amelia Earhart fan since she was four and had read about her in a book. Nellie just loved how brave Amelia was and how she was so strong and willing to try new things. She couldn't believe that she had the chance to meet one of her heroines. The time machine stopped her train of thought as it crashed to the ground.

"Welcome to Oakland, California, United States of America. The date is March 16, 1937. The local language is English. Do you need any more information?" said the computer.

"No, thanks," Nellie said.

"Turn on invisibility shield." Niles ordered.

"Invisibility shield engaged," the robotic voice chirped.

The kids giggled and stepped outside to figure out exactly where they'd landed. The city around them looked a bit like the Oakland they'd visited before. The landscape was the same. The buildings were not. It was raining. Just like it should be. Nellie went back into the time machine and pulled out a purple jacket for herself and Niles' favorite green sweatshirt for him.

Niles smiled at his sister. He should have known that she would be prepared for anything they might face. "How will we find her?" he asked.

"She's been delayed by the weather. I am sure that she's sticking close to the airport. If nothing else, someone down there will know something about Amelia and where she might be."

"You're right!" Niles agreed. They headed out of the Purple Flyer and stared down the street. After a moment, Nellie turned around and looked at the time machine, sitting there in the middle of street. It seemed unsafe, even with the invisibility shield. An alleyway was one thing, but in the middle of a city on an open street it might get damaged, and then they'd never make it home.

"Stop," she said to Niles.

"What?"

"We have to move the Purple Flyer. It's not safe here. What if someone finds it? Plus, the rain isn't good for the electronics, with or without the invisibility shield."

"You're right. Where will we put it?"

Nellie's eyes searched their surroundings under her purple rectangular frames. There were shops and businesses lining the street, but none of them made a good spot to hide the time machine. A church sat alone at the end of the street. It reminded her of the wedding and how safe she'd felt leaving the time machine there.

"The church. Is it locked?" Nellie hoped that since it was a Tuesday no one would be using the church.

They walked to the front of the brick building and tried the door. It opened. They peeked inside and called out, "Anyone here?"

No one answered. The kids walked around the building for a bit, checking the sanctuary, the corridors, and the kitchen for signs of people. They looked out a back door and saw a shed.

Niles pointed and Nellie nodded.

"That's the perfect spot."

The time machine was waiting for them where they'd left it. The Novas had installed pop-out wheels in the rebuild, and this proved to be useful. They rolled it up the street, into the church, out the back door, and to the shed. Thankfully, even with boxes and boxes of hymnals and choir robes and a lifesize nativity set, they were able to shift things around well enough to fit the time machine. They stacked a wise man on top of the Purple Flyer and closed the shed. There was a gate in the back. It led to an alley.

"When we come back, we don't have to go through the building as long as this stays open," Nellie said. They propped it with a rock and walked to the end of the alley and onto a large street.

"How are we going to get to the airport?" Niles asked.

Stephenie Peterson

"I guess we start by finding out where it is," Nellie answered.

After a short walk down the street, they found some men were waiting for a bus.

"Excuse me, sir," Niles said to the nearest man. "Could you please tell me how to get to the airport?"

The man seemed suspicious of them, likely because Nellie was dressed in jeans and a T-shirt, which was not common for a little girl in the 1930s, but he told them anyway. It was a few miles north of the bus stop.

As the siblings walked in the direction the man had indicated, Nellie's mind was full of thought. She was going to meet Amelia Earhart. Nellie wondered what she should say to the famous pilot. Nellie had always admired her for her bravery, for her skill, and for being a woman who was willing to step into what had always been a man's world. She was the first woman to fly an airplane alone across the Atlantic Ocean. Nellie imagined that must have been scary and invigorating all at once, alone in the sky over the never-ending sea. And in Amelia's time women had been treated so differently from how they were treated in Nellie's own. It must have

78

taken a lot of courage to step into such a brave role. Nellie had always admired the pilot. She knew that Amelia would go missing later this year, never to be seen again. She wanted to warn her.

"Do you think I should tell her?"

"Tell who what?" said Niles, who wasn't aware of Nellie's inner dialogue.

"Tell Amelia that she's going to go missing later this year."

Niles's face grew serious. He thought for a moment before he spoke.

"You've done something amazing here, Nellie. You've really changed the world with your time machine. So many great discoveries could be made with it. But we can't go and change history. Who knows what could happen if she doesn't get lost. I know it's hard, but we can't change the past."

Nellie's face fell. She knew he was right. She just didn't want to admit it. There's no telling what could happen if they changed the past. She knew that she couldn't tell Amelia about where and when she came from or what would happen to her in July, no matter how badly she wanted to do so.

They were approaching the airport at this point. They didn't know exactly how they were going to find Amelia, but this had to be a good place to start.

A small crowd of people was gathered outside. They slipped into the back of the group to listen.

"I wonder where Earhart plans to fly," said a middle-aged man wearing a hat and round glasses.

"Do you know where she is?" asked Nellie, surprising herself. She hadn't planned on speaking up. "I, um, walked down here hoping to get her autograph."

Several people turned around and looked at the Nova children. Niles gulped and ran his hands through his red hair. He often did this when he was nervous.

"You want to know where Amelia Earhart is?" one of the men finally inquired.

"Yes, sir," said Nellie as politely as possible.

"I heard she's having lunch at the café down the street," said the man with glasses as he pointed to a nearby restaurant.

"Thank you, sir," Nellie replied and the kids scurrled off down the road.

They approached the café with great reverence. After looking at the door for a moment too long, Nellie took a deep breath and said, "This is it." She opened the door with confidence, but her brown eyes showed her nervousness.

CHAPTER ELEVEN

The café was buzzing with conversation. Nellie and Niles breathed in smells of coffee, sausage, bacon, and toast. A waitress in a pink apron greeted the kids and told them they could sit anywhere. Amelia sat alone at a table in the back corner of the restaurant reading a newspaper. She wore a brown jacket and white blouse. Nellie thought she looked strong and beautiful all at once. Nellie walked straight for Amelia, and Niles struggled to keep up.

A funny thing happened, however, as she got to Amelia's table. All the excitement within her swelled to the point of a spiraling frenzy. Suddenly, Nellie was overcome with the moment, with having traveled through time, multiple times, with the fact that Amelia Earhart sat only a few feet away . . . all of it consumed her. When Nellie opened her mouth to speak, no words came.

Amelia took notice of the children and looked up.

"Can I help you kids?" she asked.

Niles poked Nellie, who still couldn't speak.

"My sister, Nellie, really wants to meet you," Niles told Amelia. As much as he liked to tease Nellie about her occasional shyness, he wasn't about to let it ruin the moment. She had worked so hard and come so very far for this.

"Does she?" Amelia asked.

Nellie managed to nod. Amelia smiled.

"Do you want to sit down?" she asked them.

Nellie's eyes widened. "Yes!" she squeaked. Nellie scrambled into the booth, then Niles sat down calmly.

"I think you're amazing. You paved the way for women to do so much. I can't believe all that you've done!" Nellie rambled.

"Thank you, Nellie," Amelia replied, smiling. "How old are you two?"

"Nine. And he's eleven," Nellie said, pointing to Niles. Niles nodded in agreement.

"Do you live nearby?" Amelia asked.

"Not exactly," Niles answered quickly, trying not to let his nervousness show in his voice.

"We came to find you," Nellie told Amelia.

"Well, I'm honored." said Amelia. "What do you want to be when you grow up?"

"I want to be a chemist," said Niles, relieved that Amelia did not want to know more about where they came from.

"That's great. You seem like a swell kid. And you, Nellie?"

"I'm not sure yet. Some sort of scientist, but I haven't narrowed down what I'll study. I'm interested in physics and engineering."

Amelia looked at Nellie with kind eyes and nodded. "That's a brave choice for a young girl. I think that's aces! Girls need to know they can do anything that boys can. It's so important."

Nellie just grinned. As extraordinary as she was, she was too excited to think of anything brilliant to say.

"Would you kids like to come back to the airport with me and see my plane?" Amelia asked as she set some money on the table to pay for her meal.

Nellie nodded, too overcome with excitement to speak. "Yes, please!" Niles exclaimed.

"Well, come on then," Amelia said as she rose from the table.

The kids followed her through the small café and out the door. The short walk was filled with Nellie asking Amelia about her solo flight across the Atlantic.

"Was it scary?" she asked.

Amelia nodded. "A bit, but it was invigorating."

"What made you do it?" asked Nellie.

"Women everywhere. And little girls like you. So you can be a scientist, Nellie, if that's what you want. So women can fly, in the sky or on the ground."

Nellie, being from the future, knew how much Amelia and other women like her had changed the world. She knew that while there were still a lot of jobs where the men outnumbered the women by a lot, little girls everywhere could not only dream about becoming a pilot or a scientist, they could live those dreams.

"Thank you, Amelia. For leading the way."

Amelia smiled warmly. They'd reached the airport now and were walking toward the hangar where Amelia's plane, the Electra, was waiting patiently for its next adventure.

The kids oohed and aahed over the plane. Both Nova children were in awe of the fact that they were seeing, touching, and sitting in the cockpit of Amelia's Earhart's airplane. Nellie kept thinking that she must be dreaming, but the moment was as real as real could possibly be.

The kids chatted with Amelia about the plane, the flight, about the places Amelia had flown, what it was like to be a woman in a male-dominated field, and much more. Amelia was kind and easy to talk to, and better yet, she was more than willing to share stories with the Nova kids. She told them about the Ninety-Nines, a group of female pilots she'd helped form and the interesting women she'd come to know through the organization.

After about twenty minutes, Amelia told the kids that she had to go get some rest. They thanked her over and over again.

"The pleasure was all mine, kids. You are some really amazing little people!"

Both children's cheeks turned as red as Niles' hair.

As they left, Amelia took her newspaper from earlier in the day and signed it with the following note:

"Dear Nellie and Niles,
Always remember, you can change the world.
Best Wishes,
Amelia"

They trudged through the rain back toward the church, happy to have met such an influential woman. But something didn't sit right in Nellie's magnificent mind. The gears turned to dreary music, and the books flipped slowly. Nellie felt guilty. She caught sight of Amelia's note on the newspaper, and the music within her mind picked up its pace to become a happy tune.

"She was so nice to us, and we didn't even warn her," she said to Niles as he dug through the shed where they had left the machine. It was difficult to see in the rain, and it was considerably harder than they expected to find it among the stacks of boxes within the shed. The invisibility shield wasn't help-ing matters any.

"Huh?" asked Niles, poking his head back out of the shed while struggling to pull the Purple Flyer free from underneath pieces of the nativity scene.

"It's not right," Nellie began. "I know we're not supposed to change history. But all anyone knows about Amelia is that she disappeared. What if she still disappears, but we take her somewhere safe? Sometime safe. She could go anywhere with us."

Niles was unsure. He bit his lip, took a deep breath, and opened his mouth. No words came out. He began to pace back and forth in front of the shed. He did not look up from his black-and-white Chuck Taylor sneakers while he walked. After about four laps, he opened his mouth again and still couldn't bring himself to talk.

"Niles, she told us to remember that we can change the world," Nellie reminded him. "We can't go and rescue everyone who ever met a bad fate throughout history, but we can save Amelia."

Niles paced some more. He did not like the idea of changing history, but Nellie made a valid point. He opened his mouth again. "I . . . I . . ." he stuttered. He took a long, deep breath. "I think we should do it," he told her, his voice excited yet his mind still a bit unsure.

"Yes!" Nellie squealed and jumped up and down. "Let's go!"

Niles finally managed to pull the Purple Flyer free from the shed. He pulled with a bit too much force, however, and it sent him and the time machine flying. A wise man, a donkey, and a box of choir robes flew out of the shed and landed on top of the kids. A robe drifted down to Nellie's head, covering her unruly hair like a bad hat. They laughed, picked up their mess, and pulled the Purple Flyer upright.

They got in. Nellie, who had read as much as she could get her hands on about Amelia Earhart, knew that Amelia went missing on July 2nd. Since no one knew exactly where she ended up, Nellie was going to try to get the time machine onto the plane right after Amelia's last radio call, at 8:43 a.m. Nellie put the name and location of the plane, the time, and the date into the computer.

She looked over at Niles and asked, "Are you ready?" Niles nodded with excitement.

"Let's do this!"

CHAPTER TWELVE

The Purple Flyer began to glow. As before, it started to spin, slowly at first, but it quickly picked up pace until it lifted off the ground. Nellie and Niles watched in excitement as the machine spiraled through time. This had quickly become Nellie's favorite part of time travel. They stared, awestruck as they spiraled past knights on horseback, erupting volcanoes, crashing waves, and a parade through a city. Nellie gasped as a whale jumped out of the stars and crashed down in front of them. Niles poked her side, and they giggled.

Nellie tried to prepare herself for what was about to come. Big moments in your life often come without you knowing how big they truly are beforehand. This wasn't that kind of moment. This moment was filled with the enormity of the situation. Nellie and Niles both knew that this was going to be one of the most important things they'd ever do. The mood became more solemn as the box's spiral ended, and it came to a stop inside the Electra.

Amelia screamed. Fred Noonan, who was her crew for this flight, jumped out of his seat. Nellie and Niles walked out of the Purple Flyer a bit shaken up. The computer spouted off their location.

"I don't understand what's going on," Amelia said, obviously distressed.

"Who are you?" asked Fred.

"Amelia, we met in Oakland. I'm Nellie and this is

Niles," Nellie said quickly, not knowing how much time they had. Amelia's eyes flickered with recognition.

"How did you get here? Why are you here?" Amelia asked.

"I know it's hard to understand, but this box is a machine that travels through time. We live in the year 2015. In our time, you're still very well-known, but, Amelia, a lot of what people remember is that you disappear. Today. No one ever hears from you again after that call you just made."

This may seem like a blunt way to put it, but Nellie needed to get her point across and quickly. What's a girl supposed to do when she has to get something so important across with so little time? Thankfully for Nellie, Niles, Amelia, and Fred, it worked.

Fred looked dubious, but Amelia believed them. "Something's been off all day. How do we get out of this plane?"

"Get into the box," Nellie ordered in her most commanding voice, which I have to admit wasn't especially commanding.

Fred and Amelia exchanged glances, but followed

the kids to the back of the plane, where the purple time machine stood. Amelia peeked her head in and took in her surroundings. Then she stepped in and told Fred to do the same. He did. Nellie and Niles followed.

"Where did you get this machine?" Amelia inquired, her voice filled with both suspicion and wonder.

"Nellie built it," Niles said.

Amelia raised her eyebrows and nodded in approval. Nellie blushed, her freckles standing out more than ever.

"We'll take you anywhere, anytime, except your own homes and time." Nellie told them somberly. "You're so famous throughout history as people who were never seen again. If you just magically show up at home, who knows what could happen."

Fred looked distressed, but Amelia just nodded.

"You said you live in the year 2015? I think I'd like to see that. What about you, Fred?"

"I don't know what to think. Are you sure we should do this?"

"It's that or we go down with the plane. What

other scenario ends in no one ever seeing us again?"

"And you believe these kids? I mean they are as cute as a bug's ear and that gal's loaded with moxie, but do you trust them?"

"How else did they end up on our plane like that?"

Fred sighed. "Okie-dokie, 2015 it is. Do you kids live in the States?"

"Yes, sir," said Niles.

"All right. Take us home with you."

Nellie and Niles wondered what their parents would think. But there was no time to discuss it. Nellie instructed the Purple Flyer to go home. The machine lit up. Neon green light radiated throughout the entire plane.

"Whoa!" said Fred. Niles giggled.

"Just wait," said Nellie right as the time machine began to spin.

"And I thought air travel was daring," said Amelia.

The machine spun faster and faster and lifted up into space. Fred and Amelia held back in the corner at first, but the kids encouraged them to look into the spiraling eternity outside the windows.

"It's just so beautiful," Amelia gasped.

"Oh my. It's . . it's . . ." Fred sputtered.

"It's amazing," Nellie chimed in.

"Absolutely amazing," Niles added.

"I thought I'd seen so much, flying all over the world, but I've just seen a mere speck in the vastness that is eternity," Amelia whispered, her face solemn.

They stood in silence, watching the wonder and beauty before them until the box spun haphazardly into Nellie's bedroom, hitting the ground with a bounce.

CHAPTER THIRTEEN

"Whooo-eee," yelled Fred.

"Oh my," said Amelia as she stood up.

Nellie and Niles just grinned. They were excited to show Amelia and Fred their home.

Before they could even compose themselves enough to make their way out of the box, Nellie's bedroom door flew open. Fox and Annie burst through the door.

Fox, who had been excited to hear all about their adventures, grew agitated at the sight of Fred, who had exited the box first. Fox's body tensed. His face turned as red as his hair and his hands balled up into fists. Fox wasn't a violent man, but a father's instinct to protect his family is immense.

"What is going on here?" Fox snarled, his voice louder than usual.

Fox rushed toward Fred. "Who are you and why are you in my daughter's bedroom?"

Amelia, being closer to the exit of the time machine got out next, followed by Niles, and finally Nellie.

"Amelia Earhart?" Fox sputtered. "What...how...?"

"Don't be mad, Daddy. We're okay."

"We made it to 1937 Oakland and met Amelia Earhart," Nellie said, nodding toward Amelia. "After meeting her, we knew we couldn't let her disappear, Daddy. She was so kind, so inspirational. When we got back to the time machine, I couldn't come back here knowing that she was going to be lost forever. I just couldn't. So we intercepted Amelia and Fred right after their last known radio communication, and we brought them with us," Nellie explained, waving a hand at Fred and Amelia as she spoke.

Annie and Fox turned and looked at Amelia and

Fred, dumbfounded. After an awkward moment of silence, Fox stuck out his hand and said, "Fox Nova. It's nice to meet you, Miss Earhart, Mr. Noonan."

Fred took his hand and shook it, then Amelia did the same.

"It's an honor to meet the parents of these brilliant kids," Amelia beamed.

Annie smiled and thanked her.

"So, what do we do now?" asked Frank, looking around the room. "I want to see 2015."

They started with the house, showing them advancements in technology. Cell phones, computers, tablets, Blu-ray players, and even the dishwasher were all sources of great wonder for Amelia and Fred. A lot had changed in the world in the years between 1937 and 2015, and they were eager to experience it all.

Fred was most impressed with Niles's iPod.

"Thousands of songs held in the palm of my hand! It does not even seem possible."

Amelia, however was most taken with the internet. "It is hard to believe that a gal can access so much information at any time. It's a true wonder!"

Nellie showed her photos and videos online of current-model airplanes. Amelia could not believe the improvements in aero-space engineering. While gazing at a photo of a  commercial airliner online she sighed. "I can't wait to see one of these beauties up close," she told the Nova family with a tone of reverence in her voice. "Can you imagine, Fred?" she said, turning toward her friend and partner in the sky.

"I really can't," said Fred. He seemed less enthused than Amelia.

In fact, Fred was pretty overwhelmed by all that

had happened during day. He was beginning to feel quite haggard and felt ready for sleep. The realization that he'd never see anyone he'd known and loved was starting to catch up to him. It was a horrid feeling, knowing that in his own time his loved ones were so very worried about him.

"Do you kind folks have a place I could take a rest?" he asked Fox and Annie.

"Of course, let me show you to the guest room," Annie said to him and guided him to a small room in the back of the house. The bedding and curtains were floral patterned and the walls were a cheery yellow. A small white antique nightstand with a simple lamp on it stood next to the bed. There were no computers, cell phones, or any other modern devices in the room.

"This room feels more like home," Fred said wistfully.

Annie nodded. "Please let us know what we can do to make this transition easier for you, Fred. I can't imagine what you're going through right now."

Fred forced a weak smile and sat down on the bed. "Your whole family is being wonderful. Thank you, Mrs. Nova."

Annie left him to rest. As she paced down the hall, she was overcome by the sorrowful air that had hung over Fred's room.

The next morning, Annie and Fox both called in sick to work. They were not usually the kind of people who told white lies, however you can't exactly tell your boss that you cannot come in to work because you have unexpected, time-traveling guests in your home.

Annie was especially overwhelmed by her guests. It's not that she was an unwilling host. It was quite the opposite. She was such an empathetic person that she felt their unease almost as strongly as Amelia and Fred. Honestly, it was mostly Fred who was in a state of unease. Amelia had taken to the twenty-first century like a bird takes to the sky. She was happy—a bit homesick for family and friends, but she was so filled with joy about her new experiences that she didn't dwell on it.

Fred rarely came out of the guest room. Around noon, Annie asked Nellie to bring him some food. Nellie knocked timidly on the door. "Fred?" she said in her sweet, small voice. "My mom made you some soup and a sandwich." After a moment of silence, which I must tell you was painfully awkward, Fred came to the door. His face was without expression as he took the plate from Nellie's hand. "Thank you, sweetheart," he told her. "That's very kind of you both," he said, closing the door before he finished speaking.

Nellie could not help but feel guilty. She knew it must be hard for Fred to adjust to their time. But she felt when someone disappears without an answer that nothing good ever comes of it. What-ever fate had faced Amelia and Fred, it had to have been worse than sitting in the guest bedroom of Casa Nova.

Nellie sighed sadly and walked into the kitchen, where she found Amelia and Niles sitting at the kitchen table. Niles was showing her his Kindle.

"So you just type in the name of any book you want, and you can read it immediately?" Amelia asked, her blue eyes wide with wonder.

"Pretty much," said Niles with a smile.

"That's fantastic!" She was awestruck at the amount of information available to people of the twenty-first century. She looked up and noticed Nellie standing in front of her.

"Oh, hello, Nellie!" she said cheerfully. "Niles was just showing me his e-reader. It's fascinating!"

Nellie smiled and nodded in agreement.

Fox and Annie walked into the room.

"How'd it go with Fred?" asked Annie.

"He seems really sad, Mom."

Annie and Fox exchanged a glance in the way adults tend to do when something is wrong, but they don't want their kids to know. This, of course, is this is the universal signal to kids that something is, in fact, wrong.

"Amelia," began Fox, "what should we do for Fred?"

"He seems to want to be alone for now," she answered, her smile fading.

Annie's sad eyes met Amelia's. "Hopefully, it will all seem better in a few days."

CHAPTER FOURTEEN

Time passed, as it has a way of doing, with or without access to a time machine. After about a week, Fox and Annie were back at work, Amelia had made herself quite at home, but Fred . . . Well, Fred was not doing well. He was a fish out of water in the twenty-first century, and nothing seemed to put him at ease. The sadness that hung over him was so strong it felt like you could reach out and touch it.

One day, as she passed the guest room, the door to which was, as always, closed, Nellie had an idea. It was one of her brilliant ideas that sent her phenomenal mind into overdrive. The flipping of the pages of the giant books picked up, and the ballerinas danced to a cautiously happy tune.

She still had a time machine. It was where they'd left it, standing in her bedroom. She could use it again and take Fred to a time where he'd be happier. He could never go "home," because everyone agreed that it would alter history too much, but maybe if he went back in time a bit he would be happier.

Nellie decided that Amelia was the best person to tell about her plan first. She reasoned that Amelia knew Fred best and would know if it was as good an idea as she thought. Amelia agreed that Fred's sorrow was too great, and they decided to ask Annie and Fox what they thought.

More time travel made Fox and Annie both nervous, since the last trip had brought them two permanent house guests, but they agreed that there was nothing else to be done. Fred was just too unhappy in 2015. Everyone agreed that Amelia should be the one to offer to take him to another time.

Amelia slowly made the walk to the guest room, worried about the conversation and sad that it would likely sever her last connection to her own time. She did not want to leave. She was happy in

2015 and understood why she could never go home. She knew that if Fred went to another time, he'd be doing it without her.

She let out a heavy sigh and knocked the door.

"Yeah?" Fred responded.

"It's Amelia," she replied.

"Come in."

She opened the door and walked over to the bed, where Fred was sitting.

"You're not happy here," she began.

He nodded, tears in his eyes.

"You don't have to stay, Fred. If this isn't right for you, you've got all of history to consider. I know you just want to go home, but if you can't do that, maybe another time and place would make you happier."

Fred's face softened. He had not considered using the time machine again.

"And the Novas? They don't mind?"

"Yes, Fred. Everyone wants you to be happy."

"Then I'll do it," he said, and for the first time since he had arrived in the Nova home, his face showed the faintest hint of a smile.

CHAPTER FIFTEEN

The next day, Nellie, Niles, and Fred stood next to the time machine. Annie, Fox, and Amelia were in Nellie's room, saying their good-byes to Fred. Good-byes are especially hard when you know that you'll never see someone again. It was quite an emotional scene filled with hugs, handshakes, and a few tears. In spite of the sadness of parting ways, everyone in the room felt lighter. After a bit of internet research, Fred had decided to go to England in 1961, reasoning that it was far enough in distance and time from their disappearance for him not to be recognized, but a simpler time filled with less technology.

After many rounds of hugs and tears, Fred, Nellie, and Niles got into the time machine. Nellie punched in the date and location, and the machine began its dramatic show of motion and lights. Annie gasped, Fox cheered, and Amelia smiled and let out a laugh at the sight of it all.

After the box spiraled through time for a few minutes it crashed to the ground, bouncing on its tire-covered bottom. The trio poked their heads out to find a small English village with cobblestone streets filled with cars that Nellie and Niles thought looked really, really old.

Fred turned to Nellie and Niles and said, "Thank you, kids. For rescuing us. And for this." He gestured to the town behind them. His voice softened. "I am sorry that I wasn't happy in your world. Your whole family was so kind to me," he apologized.

"You don't have to be sorry, Fred. You got pulled out of your life in an instant. You didn't have a choice and all any of us wanted was for you to be happy," said Nellie, sounding, as usual, wiser than her age.

Fred hugged the kids and stepped out of the purple box.

"Well, I expect it's time for you kids to go and time for me to make a new life. Alone," he said, his sadness showing in his eyes. "Take care of Amelia. Not that she needs It."

"Bye, Fred!" they called.

He slowly walked down the street away from them, shoulders slumped. Every movement he made seemed to be heavy with sorrow. It hurt Nellie to see him so sad. Seeing him like that made her feel the same way she'd felt when they had left James and Ruby in the 1890s.

"James and Ruby," she thought to herself. "That's it!"

"Fred! Wait!" Nellie called out gleefully.

He turned and looked at her.

"What if you don't have to be alone?"

"What do you mean?" Fred asked.

"I know some kids. Back in 1892. They don't have a family. They live on the street. They have to steal to eat. I hated leaving them behind when we met them. What if we all went and got them and brought them back here with you? You wouldn't have your family, but you wouldn't be alone, either," Nellie said excitedly as the ballerinas in her mind began to pirouette to joyful music.

Fred's face perked up. His eyes seemed to twinkle with glee.

"That sounds like a wonderful idea, Nellie!"

Nellie and Niles high-fived each other and they all headed back into the time machine, which went spiraling through time, putting on a spectacular show for Fred, Niles, and Nellie as they waited to land in 1892. Nellie set the machine to land at the same time they'd left before.

The machine landed with a thud, and Nellie turned on the invisibility shield. They ran out of the machine just as the old cardboard time machine disappeared. They could hear the men yelling at Ruby and James down the street.

"Our friends are named James and Ruby. Tell these men you're their dad. With a British accent if you can," Nellie instructed Fred as they ran toward the sound of Ruby screaming.

Niles was running fastest and got to Ruby and James first. "Hey! Wait!" he called to the men, who were trying to carry Ruby and James away. I say "trying" because the kids were really fighting them and making the task quite difficult. Fred and Nellie caught up with Niles just as the men turned around.

"What business is it of yours?" the larger man snarled.

"It's my business, sir. Those are my children," Fred told them in a perfect British accent.

Ruby's eyes went wide, but she dared not argue with him.

The men reluctantly released James and Ruby, telling Fred he should punish them for stealing. Nellie led the way back to the time machine. When they were out of earshot of the men, Ruby and James thanked Fred, Nellie, and Niles. Ruby asked

Nellie how they'd been able to change their clothes so quickly.

"I will explain that to you, but first, James and Ruby, I'd like to introduce you to my friend Fred," Niles told them.

"I hear you don't have a family," Fred said in low voice. "I don't either. Not anymore. Would you like to come live with me?"

Ruby and James were understandably surprised. They didn't talk at first. After a few moments, Ruby turned to Nellie and asked in a quiet voice, "Is 'e serious?"

"I am, Ruby," Fred answered with a smile.

Ruby looked to James, who looked to Niles. Niles nodded. James smiled broadly.

"You mean we can come with you? We don't have to steal to eat?" James asked Fred.

"Yes. You can come with me. We'll find a home together. But there's something else we'll have to explain," Fred told them.

"This is going to sound crazy," Nellie began, "but we are from the future." She walked up to the time machine and instructed it to turn off its invisibility shield. James and Ruby's eyes grew wider.

"This is my time machine. I can use it to visit any time I'd like. What I would like to do is take you to the year 1961. Fred had to start his life over in a new time. If you go with him, you can do it togeth-er."

Ruby and James seemed suspicious, but excited as well. James peered into the time machine.

"I think she's serious," he told Ruby. She nodded.

"Should we go?" Ruby whispered to her brother. He also nodded. Fred beamed.

Nellie opened the door to the Purple Flyer and motioned for everyone to follow her. She instruct-ed it to return to the village outside of London in 1961. Ruby and James were quiet. Then the machine filled with green light and started to spin. Ruby screamed. James squeezed her hand. Fred put his hand on her shoulder and told her it would be okay. The machine lifted off and began its beau-tiful journey through eternity. Ruby and James were overwhelmed with all they saw.

"This ain't a dream, innit?" Ruby asked her brother.

"I don' think it is," he answered.

Just then, outside the time machine, hundreds of butterflies flew past them.

"If this is a dream, I don' want to wake up," Ruby said wistfully.

Nellie spied the ground and warned them about the landing. "It might feel scary, but we'll be okay!"

The machine hit the ground with a bounce and announced their arrival. Everyone got out of the time machine.

"Well, I guess this is good-bye, then." Niles said.

Nellie gave hugs to Ruby, James, and Fred. "I hope you are all happy in this time."

Fred looked at Ruby and James, and smiled. "I think we will be."

"Good-bye!" Nellie and Niles said together.

"Good-bye!" Ruby and James replied cheerfully.

"Good-bye, kids!" Fred said. He inhaled happily and took hold of Ruby's and James's hands. Then they walked away, down the street and slowly out of sight.

CHAPTER SIXTEEN

Nellie and Niles landed back in Nellie's purple bedroom with a bounce. They burst out of the Purple Flyer and sprinted toward the kitchen to find their family. Both kids had a lot of feelings to process, and they wanted to share them with people who understood. They opened their mouths to tell Amelia, Fox, and Annie about taking Fred to England, but barely got a sound out before there was a knock at the door.

Annie opened the door to reveal three large men in dark suits and sunglasses—the same three men Nellie and Niles had seen twice before, lurking near Casa Nova. Nellie instantly felt uneasy at the sight

of them.

"Hello, ma'am," said the tallest of the three men as he flashed a badge. "I am Agent Jacob Riley with the National Agency for Technology and Air Travel. This is Agent Bishop," he said, pointing at the shorter, dark skinned agent, "and that's Agent Maloney." He nodded toward the blond-haired agent. "We've been tipped off to some unusual activity on radar in the vicinity of this address. Could we come in and talk?"

Annie's round eyes filled with panic as she turned to Fox, Amelia, and the kids. She didn't know what to do, so she let them in.

The Novas and Amelia tried to appear calm, but they were feeling quite uneasy. Nothing good could come of these visitors' questions.

"You must be Annie, and you're Fox," stated Agent Riley. He did not ask, he seemed to know for sure who they were. "But I don't know who you are," he said, looking to Amelia.

"She's my aunt. Auntie Amelia," said Nellie quickly. Everyone seemed to accept this. Everyone except Agent Maloney, who paused for a moment and looked at Nellie intently. Nellie's mind went into overdrive. The gears spun haphazardly and the giant books flipped with such fury that the resulting wind whooshed the ballerinas off-kilter. Nellie knew in that moment that something awful was about to happen and she felt it was up to her to fix it. But how?

"Unusual activity on radar?" asked Fox as the agents took a seat on the antique green velvet sofa. "What does that even mean?"

"Don't play coy with me, Professor Nova," said Agent Riley, who seemed to be the speaker for the group of agents. "We know you're up to something."

"Me?" laughed Fox nervously. "What am I up to?"

"Our radar has shown some very unusual activity

surrounding your home. We think you are dabbling in time travel and we're here to shut you down."

"Time travel?!" Fox scoffed. "You can't be serious. Sure, it's theoretically possible, but it's never been done. What makes you think that I am traveling in time?"

"We've seen your work, Fox. We know what you're capable of," said Agent Riley.

"Well, I have to say I am flattered, but I can assure you, I haven't left 2015 all day."

On the inside, Nellie was freaking out. She didn't know what to do. Could her father get in trouble for what she'd done? Fox made eye contact with Nellie and gave her a look, clearly trying to tell her something.

"Nellie, Niles, why don't you go play? In Nellie's room. And we'll let the agents look around the house so we can assure them that I am not hiding a time machine in the garage."

"But Dad," Nellie protested. "I don't want to play. I want . . ."

Fox gave her a look again, and suddenly it was clear. He was telling her to RUN.

Nellie and Niles went to her room. They paused to listen at the door. They heard their dad telling the agents that he would be more comfortable speaking with them if the kids were not around. Niles frowned. Nellie made a beeline for the time machine.

"What are you doing? We've got to hide that!" exclaimed Niles in an angry whisper.

"Exactly. We've got to hide it in another time. Until the agents leave. If we come back a few hours from now, they should be gone. "

Nellie and Niles climbed into the machine, and Nellie told the machine to come back to her room in two and a half hours. Off into eternity they flew.

Meanwhile, Fox, Annie, and Amelia nervously showed the agents around the house.

Fox opened the door to the garage.

"No time machine here," he said as the agents entered. They walked around the room, picking things up and tossing them aside as they went.

"Excuse me," said Annie in the most polite tone she could muster at the moment, "Please do not make a mess of my home. We've been more than polite, letting you in and showing you around and answering your questions. I would appreciate it if you could be gentler with our belongings."

Agent Maloney rolled his eyes. Agent Riley picked up a box marked "Christmas Decorations—FRAGILE," opened it, lifted it over his head, turned it over, then  dropped it to the ground. The sound of shattering glass filled the room. Annie winced, but decided not to say anything else. Amelia went pale as she realized how ruthless the agents were willing to be. Agent Bishop shot Agent Riley a look of disgust and then turned to Annie and mouthed, "Sorry." Annie nodded, tears in her eyes.

After Agent Riley finished ransacking the garage, he moved on to Fox's office. He knocked over a filing cabinet. Next came Fox and Annie's room. As Agent Riley threw all of Annie's good dresses on the floor, Agent Bishop finally spoke up.

"Is that really necessary, Riley?" he snapped.

"Shut up, Bishop," said Riley as he rested his hand on his silvery hair. He did, however, stop throwing clothes. He turned and looked out the window.

"What's in the shed out back?" he asked.

"Gardening tools, mostly," said Fox. "Annie is a botanist."

"Annie's a botanist," repeated Riley in a mocking tone as he opened the sliding glass door and headed to the backyard. Bishop gave another apologetic glance, but Maloney laughed.

Amelia opened her mouth, wanting to chew out Riley for his rude behavior, but closed it again before she spoke. She, along with Fox and Annie, had quickly learned that Agent Riley was not the kind of man you mouth off to without major repercussions. Amelia was not the kind of woman who lived in fear but, I must admit, she was scared.

Once Riley was done throwing tools around the shed, they headed back to the house.

"What's in here?" asked Agent Riley, pointing to Niles's door.

"It's my son's room," Fox told them. Riley burst into the room, ready to find something, anything of interest.

"Do you really think there's anything in a kid's room?" asked Bishop, as Riley threw the mattress off the bed.

"You never know," said Riley with a snarl.

Next, they went through the guest room.

Finally, they were in front of Nellie's room. While Fox was confident that Nellie would have got the time machine out of there, he knew her schematics and research still covered the purple walls.

"What's in that room?" Riley barked.

"It's my daughter's room. Do you really need to bother the kids? Please? I sent them in there so they wouldn't have to see all of this."

Bishop spoke up. "That's enough, Riley. Do you really think that sweet little blond-haired girl has a time machine in her room? Come on. It's got to be a false positive on the radar." He stepped in front of Nellie's door. "There's no reason to scare the kids."

Riley looked annoyed but said, "Fine. Let's go!"

He turned and looked at Fox.

"We'll be watching you, Mr. Nova."

And with that, the agents stormed out the door,

except for Agent Bishop, who kept turning around and mouthing apologies.

CHAPTER SEVENTEEN

Outside, the agents stood looking at Casa Nova.

"I don't know why you have to be like that, Riley," Agent Bishop said with a sigh.

"This family is up to something. I know it. This is far from over." Agent Riley answered.

Bishop sighed again, and the agents headed to the black town car parked in the driveway.

"Hey, guys," said Maloney, looking at his smart-phone.

"What is it?" said Riley as he sat down in the driver's seat.

"Neither Fox nor Annie have a sister or sister-in-law named Amelia. I ran a family background check earlier. The kid seemed funny when she called that lady Auntie."

"Well then who is that woman?" asked Bishop as they pulled out of the driveway.

"I don't know," said Riley. "But I can promise you that I will find out. I knew that they were hiding something."

Inside, Fox, Annie, and Amelia sat in the living room in silence, each of them overwhelmed by different aspects of the reality they were facing. Annie was worried that Nellie and Niles were traveling in time again. Fox was terrified that the agents would figure out what Nellie had done. Even if there were no legal issues surrounding time travel, he feared that they would take her technology and she would never get the credit she deserved for her discovery. He also worried what they might use it for if they took it. A time machine could be a terrible weapon in the wrong hands. Amelia was afraid that she would be found out, and worrying about her future. Surely, she could not just live out the rest of her life as a houseguest.

After several minutes of uncomfortable silence,

Annie spoke.

"What are we going to do?" she asked.

"I don't know. Maybe they'll leave us alone?" Fox replied with doubt in his voice.

"I don't think that is going to happen," answered Annie.

"Agent Riley seemed very determined," Amelia noted.

"Is it even a crime to travel in time?" asked Annie.

"I can't imagine it's actually in the law, no. What I think they want is to take the time machine for their own use," Fox speculated aloud.

There wasn't much time for discussion, because just then they heard a thud from Nellie's bedroom. Annie, Fox, and Amelia rushed to see how the kids' journey in time had gone.

Nellie and Niles burst through the doorway of the time machine as the adults entered her bedroom.

"What happened? Are they gone?" Nellie asked breathlessly.

"Yeah, is everyone okay? That one agent seemed

like he was out to get us!" said Niles before anyone could answer.

"Everyone's fine," Annie said, but the kids could read the worry on her face.

"What's wrong?" asked Nellie. "Something is wrong. I can tell."

"Well, they were not exactly courteous as they went through our home. They broke some things. And I think they will be back," Fox told them.

"Well, what should we do?" Nellie asked in a small, scared voice.

"I don't know," her father told her honestly as he took her hand in his. "But we will get through this together."

Annie nodded. Amelia put her hand on Nellie's shoulder. Even Niles momentarily rested his hand on hers in a sign of support.

"I hope so," said Nellie. "I really do."

CHAPTER EIGHTEEN

Everything was quiet around Casa Nova for a few
days. Nellie packed up her research and put it in
binders so it would be less obvious if the agents
came back. She labeled the binders as if they were
schoolwork. They were marked with labels such as
"History" and "Language Arts." She then put them
in a box in the back of her closet.

The time machine itself was a bit harder to hide.
Even with the mirrored shield in place, it seemed
obvious something was in her room. They moved it
to the tree house, hoping no one would look there.
She tried to move on with her normal life. She read
a lot. Mostly about all the amazing women she

wished she could use the time machine to meet. But everyone agreed it wasn't the time to use it.

After about a week, life seemed almost normal at Casa Nova. Amelia settled into the guest room. The Novas made it very clear that she was family now and she needed to relax and try to make herself at home—both in Casa Nova and 2015. She desperately wanted to try to fly airplanes again, and the Novas were trying to help her figure out how to get certified.

Niles was back to his old self. Eight days after the agents had been at their home, Niles came up with another elaborate prank. He created a collection of stink bombs, each with its own terrible smell. He rigged them to go off in a chain, starting at the garage and winding in and out of every room of the

house. Every room, that is, except for his own. He planned to get together with a friend from the neighborhood, exited Casa Nova through the garage, and set them off on the way out. He walked down the street smiling his "I'm up to no good" smile, quite proud of his mischief. When he got home and Annie told him he was grounded from video games for a month, Niles felt that it was totally, entirely worth it.

For a few days, Annie watched out the window frequently, expecting to see the agents parked across the street or walking up the driveway, but after days passed with no contact, she had started to think that the agents were going to leave her family alone. She stayed busy working, helping the kids with their schoolwork, and trying to help Amelia settle into life in 2015.

The only person who was not feeling better about the whole situation was Fox. Of course, no one in his family knew that. Fathers are like that, you know. They don't want their families to know when they are upset or worried. They want to seem strong all the time, even when they don't feel strong. The problem was, Fox didn't feel strong at all. He was really worried about what would happen if the agents found the Purple Flyer. He constantly felt like someone was watching him, even though he had no evidence to indicate that he was being observed. Fox was a man of science, a man who usually based his feelings on facts and not fear. This time, however, he could not find a way to calm his nerves. It seemed that with every passing day, the worry only became greater.

Fox started to research the National Agency for Technology and Air Travel. He read countless stories online about people who'd had run-ins with the group. Their stories were not comforting. Agents were known to cause damage to personal property, like they had at Casa Nova. They were also known to go to great lengths to get their hands on technology they thought the government could use in some way. They broke into homes, stole property, and, in one terrifying story, kidnapped an inventor and held him against his will until he revealed his secrets. The more Fox read, the more horrified he became. Still, he didn't tell his family his fears.

Twelve days after the agents had ransacked his home, Fox saw them again. It wasn't paranoia or fear; he actually saw them. He was walking to his office on the university campus to get some files before he taught a class. This was not part of his normal routine; usually, he went straight to the classroom when he got to work. He was down the hall about fifty yards from his office when he saw Agent Riley leaving it. Shocked, Fox stopped dead in his tracks. A moment later, Agent Bishop left Fox's office, followed by Agent Maloney. Fox ducked into a classroom as they turned and started making their way through the crowded hallway. His heart pounded the way it does when you've just seen a car accident or come close to being injured. He tried to catch his breath as he watched out the window to see if they would pass by or if they'd seen him. Thankfully, they did not seem to know he was there and they kept walking. Fox let out a sigh of relief and then realized that there was a lecture taking place in the classroom. He turned beet red, apologized, and left the room as quickly as possible.

Fox rushed towards his office, struggling to breathe as if fear itself were sitting upon his lungs. As he approached, he could tell even before opening the door that the agents had been as uncaring with his office as they had been to his home. Papers filled the hallway. Important parts of Fox's research, scattered,

stepped on, torn by passersby. He scooped up some files as he walked toward the door to his office, feebly hoping the work could be saved.

When he opened the door, he saw that the agents had caused quite a bit of damage. It seemed to Fox that the agents wanted to upset him as much as they wanted to find evidence of time travel. Framed photos of his family were thrown on the ground, glass shattered. His computer monitor was broken, and his hard drive was removed. Someone had pulled keys off the keyboard and spelled out "LIAR" on his desk with them. Fox was filled with a dreadful combination of fear and rage. Suddenly, a

 feeling of worry for his family filled him with a crushing, terrible sense of

unease. He canceled his afternoon classes, but there was no time to find a sub for his first class of the day. It started in less than ten minutes. He took a deep breath and assured himself that the kids were safe at home with Amelia.

He couldn't have been more wrong.

CHAPTER NINETEEN

Back at Casa Nova, Nellie was in the backyard sitting on a bench and reading a book about differential equations. Niles was in his room practicing the violin, and Amelia was in the living room researching how to create a new identity. To them, it seemed to be a normal day. They didn't notice when the black town car parked down the street. They did not hear when the three agents got out of the car. They did not startle when the men walked down the sidewalk toward their home. No one realized anything was wrong until Nellie was grabbed from behind. But even then, no one heard her screams over Niles's violin.

I don't have to tell you that Nellie tried to fight
them off. As you know, Nellie Nova was not the
kind of girl who gave up easily, not in the least. She
was as tenacious as a nine-year-old girl with unruly
blond hair can be. She kicked. She screamed. She
bit Agent Riley so hard that he bled. But in the end,
not even the most exceptional nine-year-old girl
can overpower three grown men. They dragged
her, kicking and screaming, all the way down the
street and into the town car. When Mrs. Jacobson,
who lived two houses down from the Novas, tried
to question them, Agent Maloney just flashed his
badge and she backed off.

Once in the car, they tied a gag around Nellie's
mouth to quiet her screaming and handcuffed her
to the seat. She had nowhere to go and no way to

call for help. Terror filled her small frame, and her heart rate picked up pace. She kept running different scenarios through her most exceptional mind, trying to think her way out of this awful situation. She was not coming up with any way out, however, and fear was getting the best of her. Fear is a terrible little monster because it gets in the way of innovation. It convinces you that you aren't as capable as you really are, and if you let it, it can stop you from doing great things. Nellie let fear get in her way for exactly seven minutes. Seven minutes of crying and worrying that she'd never see her family again. That's all it took for Nellie to realize something very important.

The agents were stronger, but she was smarter.

Nellie's body relaxed, and she made a mental note to pay attention to her surroundings. She noticed that they'd gone over the Owen Avenue drawbridge, which meant that they were on the east side of the Eden River. She took note of all the street names, committing them to memory. When they pulled up to an abandoned warehouse, she knew exactly where she was. She knew that it would be important to be able to find her way out of this neighborhood quickly, should the opportunity arise.

When the car stopped, they undid one side of the handcuffs to free her from the seat, and Nellie thought for a brief moment that she might have her chance to escape, but they quickly cuffed her again and held her by the chain as they forced her to walk into the building. Inside, they brought her to a small room that must have been an office at one point. They forced her to sit on a decrepit old brown upholstered chair. And finally, after twenty minutes of silence from the agents and more squealing from Nellie, Agent Riley spoke.

"I bet you're wondering why you're here, aren't you, Nellie?"

Nellie had a pretty good idea as to why, but she played along and nodded.

"We think your daddy built something dangerous, Nellie," he said in a sugary-sweet voice. "If he did, he could hurt people. If he did, the government

needs to take it away. Did your daddy make a new invention, Nellie? Something that seems really important?"

Nellie shook her head.

"Come on now, Nellie," Riley said, already sounding

exasperated. "Tell us what your daddy's built."

"He doesn't have any big projects of his own right now. It's midterms and he's busy with his students at the university. He usually does most of his research projects in the summer when he's not teaching," Nellie told them. She was trying to mask her excitement. The agents still thought Fox was the one who had made the time machine. They were merely using her to get to him. They must have been pretty desperate and out of ideas to kidnap a nine-year-old. Her clever mind started to kick into high gear.

"Now, now, Nellie," Agent Maloney said in the annoyingly sweet tone people use with dogs and babies. "I'm sure you know that it's against the law to lie to us. We're just like police officers, only even more important. Do you know what a police officer is, Nellie?"

"I'm nine," Nellie answered flatly.

"So you understand that you have to do what we say, right?"

"I understand that you can't question me without a parent or legal guardian's consent because I am a minor. That means I'm under 18," she said, matching his cloying tone.

Maloney turned red in the face with anger, but he stayed quiet for a few moments.

Nellie's mind was swirling with ideas as to how she would get out when she noticed something quite obvious. It was so simple that she'd overlooked it, and, as it turned out, so had the agents. Nellie noticed it when she tried to shift in her chair to get more comfortable. Her handcuffs were loose. So loose that her wrist slipped out ever so slightly when she moved her arm. All she had to do was wait until they all left the room, and she could easily wiggle her way out of the handcuffs. She tried to stay calm.

Agent Riley was clearly annoyed by Nellie's last remark.

"You think you're smart, don't you, kid?" he snarled.

Nellie knew she was smart, however, she was not going to admit that to Agent Riley. She looked at him and shrugged.

"You need to tell us right now what your father is up to," Riley barked.

"Well, last I saw him, he was driving to the university to teach Physics 101 to a bunch of freshmen. Does that help?" Nellie answered.

"You know that's not what I mean. Has your father built a time machine?"

"Honestly, sir, I don't know where you get these ideas," Nellie answered with a sigh. This could go on for a while. She was going to have to speed this up. But how?

"Nellie. You're breaking the law by lying to us," Agent Riley said.

"We've been over this. You're breaking the law by keeping me here," Nellie said.

Just then, she had an idea. If she could convince the agents to leave the building, she might have a chance to get away.

"I just wanna go home!" she wailed.

"Tell us the truth, Nellie. Does your dad have a time machine?" Maloney asked.

"Actually," she began, "you're right. My dad did build a time machine. But he's not keeping it at our house anymore. He's keeping it in a storage unit on Maple Street."

Maloney raised his eyebrows. Riley nodded. Bishop stood in the back of the room with his arms crossed. Agent Riley pulled out a notebook.

"Do you know what unit it's in?" asked Agent Riley.

"It's in 207-b," Nellie lied. "Can I go home now?"

"We'll see, Nellie. Agent Maloney and I have to go and see if you're telling the truth," Riley told her. "Agent Bishop will stay here with you."

Nellie thought that sounded perfect. One agent would be easier to evade than three. Riley and Maloney ran out the door quickly. Nellie hung her head and pretended to cry.

"Now, come on, kid," Agent Bishop said nervously. "Don't cry. I hate when kids cry."

Nellie continued her fake sob, making sure to keep her head down so that he would not see that no tears were falling from her face. Bishop stood up and paced back and forth in front of Nellie. He couldn't stand to see kids cry; he had a niece and nephew he loved like his own and somehow it always reminded him of them. It upset him to have to see her in distress.

"I . . . just . . ." she bawled. "I . . . just . . . need . . .

a . . . tissue!"

"Okay, okay, it will be alright." Bishop said. "I'll see what I can do about a tissue."

He walked out of the room quickly, clearly relieved to get away from the crying child. He grumbled to himself about his frustration in being left behind with Nellie while the other agents checked the storage unit.

Nellie got to work right away and within a minute or so had her hands free. Unfortunately, Agent Bishop was back before she had a chance to get out of the room. She was still sitting when he walked in the door.

"I . . . need . . . water!!" she sobbed when she saw him. He turned around without speaking.

As soon as he was out of sight, Nellie flew out of her seat and ran for the door, which, thankfully, was not locked. She stood in the open doorway for a moment before running out into the sunlight, finally free.

Or so she thought.

Right as she made it to the main street, the black town car, driven by Agent Riley rounded the corner. Riley and Maloney hopped out of the car, leaving it running in the intersection.

"Hey kid!" Riley screamed. "Didn't you think we'd figure out that there isn't a storage unit on Maple?"

Nellie ran as quickly as she could. She realized that she was not going to be able to outrun them for long. She was going to have to use her brain to get out of this one.

She kept running, but made a point to scan her surroundings for anything that could help her escape. She noticed a bike leaning up against a wall and grabbed it, feeling guilty for taking something that didn't belong to her. She hoped the bike would speed her up enough to put some distance between her and the agents. She peddled west as quickly as she could.

The agents ran behind her for a few minutes, but she proved to be too fast on bike to catch on foot, and they quickly turned around to go get their car.

Nellie's heart pounded in her chest. She came to the Owen Avenue drawbridge and was relieved to see she was headed the right direction. She flew over the bridge on the bike. Behind her, she saw the black town car round a corner. This is when Nellie was blessed with a stroke of good luck. The lights on the bridge began to flash, and a barrier went up, preventing the agents from getting on the bridge, which was opening to let a large boat pass through the river. The whole process would take several minutes, giving Nellie time to lose them. She rode her borrowed bike a few more blocks, then ditched it. She ran several blocks through alleyways, then she ducked into a restaurant.

Panting, she darted to the back of the building. A waitress gave her an odd look, and she said, "I really need to use the restroom!" and ran into the bathroom to hide out for a bit and create a plan.

"Think, Nellie!" she told herself under her breath. She was at least two miles from home, and even if she made it home, the agents would surely look for her there. She paced back and forth on the lemon-yellow tiled floor of the bathroom.

If only she could call home, she knew her family could help her. Nellie realized that the agents had probably put a tap on all their family phones, and any call she made would be intercepted. How could she get a message home?

She heard a commotion outside the restroom.

Agent Riley's gruff voice boomed through the door.

"Anybody seen this kid?" he growled. Nellie correctly assumed that he had a photo of her and was showing it to the employees and customers. Nellie could not make out the responses that murmured through the door, but she decided it would be a good idea to find her way out of the restaurant quickly.

She climbed on top of the toilet and squeezed herself out of the small rectangular window that was above it.

She dropped down into the alleyway behind the restaurant and took in her surroundings. To her left was a busy street, to her right a shopping complex. Directly in front of her was the dumpster. She heard footsteps in the parking lot and jumped into the bin.

She tried as hard as she could not to cough, gag, or breathe loudly. The smell was absolutely atrocious. It was every bit as awful as you probably think, and maybe even a bit more so. Nellie was miserable. But she was clever. The footsteps were those of Agents Riley and Maloney, who, upon finding the alley empty, decided she must have taken off on foot.

"You head east, I'll go west," Riley ordered Maloney. Nellie waited until she heard their footsteps leaving before she popped out of the trash bin.

She sighed and wondered how on earth she was going to get out of this latest terrible situation. Still half in the dumpster, she looked down at her feet to see if she had stable footing before she jumped out. What she saw excited her. Not the old food, of course, but there were several discarded mechanical items in the dumpster. Most nine-year-old girls wouldn't even take notice, but you know by now that Nellie was not like most nine-year-old girls. Nellie gathered an old cell phone, a remote-control airplane, a laptop with a cracked screen, a rundown lawn mower, and a set of rusty tools and saw them as a solution to her problem.

Inside her mind, the giant book pages flipped quickly as massive blueprints of her new machine were drawn up with colossal pencils, leaving a trail of glitter behind as they moved. The classical music in her mind picked up the tempo as all the pieces moved together to create a way to get a message home.

Nellie huddled down in the dumpster, trying not to be bothered by the awful smell, and went to work. About forty-five minutes later she'd rigged up the remote-control airplane with some of the parts from the lawn mower, hoping to increase its speed. She'd attached the cell phone so she could use its GPS to track the plane's flight with the cracked laptop. She used the Wi-Fi signal from the restaurant. She pawed through the trash and found a tattered red ribbon, which she used to attach the note to her contraption.

She took a deep breath and turned on the remote control for the airplane, thankful that the batteries seemed to have a decent charge. The airplane responded fairly well to the controls, in spite of the change in weight. She was easily able to guide it up above the building. She took it up another twenty-five feet or so to try to account for any taller structures that the plane might encounter along the way. She pointed her plane toward home and prayed a silent prayer that it would make its way home in one piece and her family would actually get her note.

Her stomach filled with butterflies as the plane flew out of sight. It was up to luck and GPS now.

CHAPTER TWENTY

Fox got home about an hour after Nellie went missing. No one had noticed her absence. Niles had stayed busy with his violin, and Amelia had found a new lead on obtaining a passport under an assumed name. They'd been absorbed in their projects and assumed that Nellie was still reading.

When Fox got home, however, he wanted to know exactly where everyone was. After Nellie didn't come in when he called, he headed outside. He saw Nellie's book askew on the ground and the overturned bench and knew something was very wrong.

"Nellie," he called nervously. "Are you up in the tree house? I need you to come down right now, sweetie."

When he heard no reply, he felt as if he'd been punched in the stomach. Trying to remain calm, he climbed up the ladder to the tree house to check if she was there. She wasn't.

He climbed down the ladder and went to the front yard. No Nellie. He walked up and down the streets of the neighborhood calling for her. Finally, he went back home and told Niles and Amelia the awful news.

"Nellie's missing. Niles, call your mother. She needs to come home right away."

"What? What do you mean she's missing?" Niles asked, confused.

"I think those agents took her. They made a mess of my office this morning. I saw them leaving campus as I got there."

"Are you sure she's not in the tree house, Dad?" Niles asked, the fear in his voice almost tangible.

"Yes, I'm sure. I've been through the whole neighborhood. Please call your mother, now."

"What can I do, Fox?" Amelia asked with worry in her eyes.

"I don't know. I really don't know," Fox replied sadly.

Twenty minutes later, they met Annie in the driveway. Fox, Amelia, Niles, and Annie talked through their options for forming a search party. They were debating who should stay home when Annie heard a noise.

"Quiet, everyone," she said. "I hear something."

Annie scanned the sky for a moment and then saw the jalopy of an airplane that Nellie had made, flying straight at Casa Nova. It began to soar lower and lower in the sky until the engine stopped right above their heads and it dropped into the front yard, a few feet from the house.

Everyone ran over to the plane to inspect it.

"What's with the ribbon?" asked Niles.

"I think there's a note attached," said Amelia.

"It's Nellie," said Annie, before she even untied the note. A mother knows her child, and Annie knew that Nellie would not make an easy hostage.

She unrolled the paper and read it.

"She's behind the Peach Tree Diner downtown. In a dumpster!"

"Let's go get her!" said Fox excitedly.

Annie rushed inside to get her keys. She set the plane down on the kitchen counter, grabbed her purse and the keys, and sprinted to the driveway.

All four of them hopped into the minivan and headed to town. A few blocks away from the restaurant, Niles called out in shock.

"It's them! It's the agents!" he said as they passed the black town car they'd come to know all too well.

"Did they see us?" Annie asked from behind the wheel.

Fox turned in his seat just in time to see the agents make a U-turn in the street.

"They did. Step on it, baby!"

Annie knew that she had to lose them before she could go rescue Nellie. She drove as fast as she could, making turns to get as far from Nellie's hide out as possible. The town car picked up its speed as well. After several miles, Annie found her way to the highway. She got on and drove six miles farther before she lost sight of the town car. She exited the highway and got back on, going the other direction.

"I think we lost them!" Amelia said, full of relief.

"I hope we have!" said Annie.

"I'll keep watch for them," said Fox. "Niles, you keep your eyes peeled too!"

They drove back toward the diner in a nervous silence. After about fifteen minutes they were in the alley. Fox hopped out of the car and knocked on the dumpster.

"Nellie? Are you there?" he whispered.

He waited nervously for what seemed like an eternity (but was only a few seconds) before Nellie popped out of the dumpster. He grabbed her, relieved to have his daughter safe again.

"I thought I'd lost you, but you're too strong for that, aren't you?" he asked her.

"I wasn't going to let them hurt us, Daddy," she replied.

She got in the car with her family. They all embraced her and the car was full of joy. The drive home was short, and everyone was still excited. That is, until they pulled onto their street and saw the familiar town car in the driveway.

"What do we do?" asked Annie. "Should I turn around?"

"No," Nellie told her. "I have a plan.

CHAPTER TWENTY-ONE

Annie parked the minivan in the street and all the Novas and Amelia nervously exited. Nellie walked right up to agent Riley and said, "I'm ready to tell the truth."

Riley's eyes went wide, and Maloney smiled. Agent Bishop looked surprised. Fox and Annie exchanged a glance, wordlessly wondering what their daughter was up to now.

"I did it," she said.

"You did what?" asked Riley.

"I made the time machine. I confess."

"You? You made a time machine?" asked Maloney.

"Yes, sir. I'll go get it. Niles, can you help me?" she asked her brother.

Niles followed her into the house.

"What are you doing?" he asked.

"Fooling them," she whispered.

A few minutes later, Nellie and Niles returned to the driveway with the purple refrigerator box that used to hold the mechanism of the old time machine. Nellie had quickly attached the remote-control airplane to the top of the box and then written "Time Machine" on it with a marker, in her sloppiest handwriting for good measure.

"What exactly is this?" asked Agent Riley.

"My time machine. I built it all by myself. Isn't it pretty?" asked Nellie, pretending to be proud of a box with a toy plane attached to it.

Agent Riley peeked into the refrigerator box, followed by Agent Maloney.

"Does this thing actually fly?" asked agent Riley.

"Oh yes, but it's not ready for human missions yet.

I took my dolly to ancient Egypt though. She met Cleopatra," said Nellie in her sweetest possible voice.

"This thing flying around the neighborhood might just set off the radar alerts," said Agent Bishop. "At that weight it might not be large enough to show up constantly, causing blips on the radar like you thought time travel would do." He looked at Riley.

Riley didn't know what to think. He just stood in the driveway shaking his head.

"I think it's time to let this one go, Riley," Agent Bishop told him. "And apologize to the Nova family for all that we've done."

Riley didn't speak. He just nodded. He felt like an idiot.

"We are just so sorry," Agent Maloney said, his eyes wide.

"I cannot apologize enough," said Agent Bishop.

Riley just kept shaking his head. The three men got in the car and drove away, leaving Nellie and her family grinning in the driveway.

CHAPTER TWENTY-TWO

Over the next few weeks, life returned to normal. Annie and Fox went to their offices, the kids worked on their schoolwork and made lots of messy art projects, and Amelia managed to get a new ID card and was able to enroll in a flight academy, where the staff was shocked at her "natural ability." She was now known as "Amelia Nova" instead of Amelia Earhart, and as far as anyone knew, she was Fox's sister.

Nellie really missed time travel. She knew she

couldn't risk the Purple Flyer showing up on radar, so it stayed parked in the tree house. She confessed to Niles just how much she missed it one day as they were working on a physics experiment in the backyard.

A few weeks later, Nellie made her way into the tree house to visit the Purple Flyer. She did this frequently. She just went out and sat in it and remembered. When she opened the door this day, however, she found Niles already inside.

"What're you doing here?" she asked. "You startled me!"

"Well, Nellie," said Niles as a smile spread across his thin lips, "I couldn't stand to see you mope around the house anymore. I had to do something. So I did some research on scrambling radar signals, and now, long story short, the Purple Flyer is untraceable. I just finished installing the radar blocker. She's ready to fly."

Nellie gasped. She threw her arms around her brother. "Thank you so much!" she squealed with delight. Nellie gasped. She threw her arms around her brother.

"Thank you so much!" she squeaked with delight.

"No problem, Sis," he replied.

"I wanted to travel in time again too. Besides, don't you have some more important women to introduce me to? I can't imagine that one world-changing woman is enough to prove your point." Joy exuded from his freckled face.

"All right!" Nellie yelled. "Let's go!"

After a quick trip inside to tell their parents that they were going to safely travel in time (they had, after all, promised to tell them if they left the house), Nellie and Niles ran back to the Purple Flyer. They stood in front of it, excitedly thinking of all the time and places they could visit.

Nellie sighed a happy sigh.

"It's like coming home," she gushed.

Every bone in her body radiated pure bliss as she started up the time machine's computer.

Nellie ordered the machine to take off. Green lights filled the tree house. The Purple Flyer began to spin, faster and faster until it took off into the spiraling vastness of time. Niles whooped. Nellie squealed with glee. They soared into eternity, ready for whatever came next.

 THE END

ABOUT THE AUTHOR

Semi-nomadic, Stephenie and her family currently live near Raleigh, North Carolina. Her kids are Texans at heart (Hi, McKinney!) and Steph and her husband grew up just outside of Seattle (What up, Port Orchard?!) Stephenie writes, creates art, and homeschools her three amazing kids. Stephenie loves to hike with her family and drink lots and lots of coffee.